THE UNICORN HERD

THE GRIFFIN SANCTUARY
BOOK 1

ARIZONA TAPE

STORIES THAT STICK

You can keep up to date with news about releases and deals by subscribing to Arizona Tape's newsletter or joining her reader group, Rainbow Central.

Caring for unicorns isn't all rainbows and sunshine.

Animal lover and keeper-in-the-making Charlotte couldn't be more excited to start her apprenticeship at the Griffin Sanctuary. Working with the unicorns is a dream come true, even if she's just a glorified stablehand at the moment. It's all worth it when she gets to help a rescued unicorn without a horn settle in.

However, she's not the only one willing to put up with the demanding hours of working at a mythical zoo. Rival apprentices from elite schools all want jobs at the Griffin Sanctuary too and Charlotte will have to use all her wits to keep her place as a unicorn keeper.

-

The Unicorn Herd is book 1 in the modern fantasy

Griffin Sanctuary series. It is packed full of adventure, mythical creatures, and a sapphic romantic sub-plot.

If you enjoy mythical creatures, zoo documentaries, slow burn sapphic romantic sub-plots, and a heroine who loves animals, you're going to love this series.

ONE

Not everyone was qualified to work with unicorns. That was why getting an internship at the Griffin Sanctuary was a dream come true. A hard-earned dream, but standing in front of the large entry gates, made it all worth it.

It was so early, they weren't officially open to visitors and yet, there was a small group of other people waiting at the gates. Something about their demeanour told me they weren't here to visit the animals.

I steadied my breathing as I joined the group. "Hi. Are you here for the internship too?"

The tallest of the girls with a blonde braid down her side gave me a steel look. "Duh."

The guy next to her chuckled as he held out his hand. "We are. I'm Aaron. How are you?"

I rushed to shake his hand, glad one of them seemed friendly. "Hey, I'm Charlotte. I'm good, thanks." Not sure how to greet the others, I gave a collective wave. "Hey, everyone."

The rude girl just rolled her eyes but the other four mumbled greetings back, although it didn't look like they were in the mood to socialise. One of the other girls was glued to her phone and the second guy seemed too nervous to talk.

Interesting group.

"Why are we waiting out here?" I questioned nervously. Opportunities like this only came around once in a lifetime and I was terrified of screwing it up. Nothing and nobody was going to get in between me and my dream job working with rare and nearly-extinct animals.

The tall girl scoffed and adjusted the strap of her fancy handbag. "The gates are locked, duh?"

"Ah, I see. Oh, there's someone coming," I pointed out, stepping to the side so I could get a better look at the woman coming to meet us.

A slightly larger woman with wiry red hair and a blue uniform waved as she opened the gates and approached our little group. "Good morning, everyone. Are you all here for the internship?"

"I am!" the tall girl chirped before anyone else could answer. She rushed through the two guys so she could shake the woman's hand first. "Thank you so much for your time."

"No problem. I'm Gwen, one of the head-keepers. Come along."

The group set in motion and I positioned myself in Aaron's vicinity. He seemed nice and I'd much rather chat with him than the rude girl.

"So which school are you from?" I asked as we passed under the large banner.

"Evergreen University," he responded, looking happy to chat.

"Wow, that's a good school. I applied there but wasn't accepted," I muttered, wishing I hadn't asked. It still stung that I didn't pass the veterinarian entrance exam but it no longer mattered. I was here.

I rubbed my arm to hide my discomfort and instead of furthering the conversation, looked around to check out the place. It was just like I remembered it from the visits with my mum.

There was a small but colourful gift shop to the left and a large, sparkling fountain graced the middle of the square. Information boards were scattered all over the place with cute pictures about the animals in the Sanctuary and fun facts. I spotted an arrow leading towards the dragon exhibit, another to the sphinx habitat, and many more that I didn't have time to read but I knew by heart where they all went.

Gwen paused near the fountain where a handful of other people in uniform were waiting. I glanced at the coins shimmering in the water. As a child, I'd tossed one in every time we visited and finally, my dream had come true.

A tan man with a curly beard handed a stack of folded maps to the tall girl. "Pass those around. You'll all do well to study the layout of the Sanctuary. The service routes and staff areas are marked on there as well."

I shifted my weight from left to right, eager to get my hands on one of those maps. The stack was half-gone by the time I had it and I passed the rest on to the guy behind me.

Only half-listening to Gwen, I flipped the map open and scanned the various pictures and habitats. We'd just passed the entrance and were standing at the wishing fountain.

I glanced at the map, noticing it had many a whole bunch of areas that I'd never seen. From the wishing fountain, three paths led to different zones of the Sanctuary and a bunch of cleverly hidden staff areas. What looked like an innocent hedge was actually a disguised entrance to the primary staff facilities. The cafeteria, the vet surgery, and the nursery were all tucked away mere meters from the public.

The red-headed woman checked her clipboard. "All seven of you are starting your internships in various zones. We've assigned you based on your expertise and current studies."

I crossed my fingers inside my pocket. Not tall girl, not tall girl.

"Felicity, Aaron, and Charlotte. You're going to the unicorn house with Nissan," Gwen read, pointing to the man with the beard.

"That's me," the tall girl chirped, stepping forward with the same confidence as before.

So I'd have to work together with her after all. Shame, but not enough to ruin my good mood. I got to help out with the unicorns, arguably one of the coolest animals around.

"And me," Aaron announced, pushing through the group to join Felicity in the front. "The unicorns are in good hands with me."

Wow. We hadn't even been here an hour and there was already a fight for who would be the teacher's pet. I shouldn't have expected anything else, only the best of the best got accepted to internships like this.

To my annoyance, I wrestled through the other people so I could be at the front too. If only I could be more laid back and let the two others be, except I wasn't going to make an impression that way. "I'm Charlotte. So excited to start."

I could feel that my beaming positivity was rubbing Felicity up the wrong way but I didn't care. Everyone knew the field of animals was cutthroat and only the best of the best would get amazing jobs like this. It was an amazing opportunity just to get this internship and I would make sure it would lead to a job offer after we were done.

Gwen ran a hand through her red hair and smiled. "That's great to hear. Nissan, I'll leave these three in your care."

The man gave us a warm smile. "Follow me."

Felicity and Aaron hurried after him like chicks following their mother hen and I was no different. Maybe I hadn't studied at the prestigious Evergreen University but my school was decent enough and I was at the top of my class. I wasn't any less qualified than these two and I was ready to prove it.

TWO

I soaked in the sights of the Sanctuary as I followed Nissan to the unicorn habitat. The paths were covered with bark chippings and wound around beautiful flower beds and large trees. Colourful signs with directions hung in convenient places and helped navigate the winding paths.

I loved it. Far beyond nostalgia, it was a wonderful place. The smell of nature and animals made me giddy and excited. Considering a job like this would take up most of my time, that was a good thing.

"Here we are. You'll be doing your internship with the silver blush unicorns since they're the easiest to work with," Nissan announced, halting in front of a locked gate. He grabbed the plastic badge hanging from his breast pocket and pressed it against the scanner. A green light flicked on and with a grin, he let the badge snap back. "There are staff-only areas everywhere on the grounds, hidden from the public eye. You'll learn to find them pretty quickly. If you're having trouble remembering, check your map."

He held the gate open for us and Felicity rushed through, beating me to it.

"After you," Aaron said, stepping aside.

"Thanks," I replied, smiling at him. At least one of them was a gentleman.

The bark chippings turned into a stone path that led us around the back of a wooden building. A familiar, musky smell hung around the premises and as Nissan opened the sliding door, the smell only grew stronger.

"You're in luck, the unicorns haven't left yet," he said as he walked into the stable.

"Do the unicorns always sleep inside?" Felicity asked as we followed him in.

Nissan grabbed a clipboard hanging by the entrance and nodded. "Yes. The lead mare brings them here every night. We check every individual's health and note it down on here," he said, tapping the clipboard. "It also gives us time to safely clean and check the habitat. Six unicorns produce a lot of shit."

Was it wrong that I was excited to see unicorn poop? Not as excited as I was to see the unicorns themselves though. I'd been wanting to see one for as long as I could remember but they were so endangered, they'd earned the status 'mythical'.

I stepped inside the stable, taking in a deep breath. Ever since I was a child, I loved the dry smell of hay. There was a hint of unicorn poop but due to their diet of plants, it always had a grassy, herby smell. Not pleasant, not unpleasant.

My heart pounded and my mouth was dry as a desert as I approached the fence. From here, I could see the sandy habitat and the beautiful wonders living in it.

In my opinion, there was nothing more majestic than the slender head and deep, sparkling eyes of a silver blush unicorn. And here at the Griffin Sanctuary, they didn't just have one, they had six. A relatively small number compared to their usual size in the wild but after all the poaching, even the largest herds had been thinned out.

I scanned the open feeding area, taking in the sight. A large white male stood closest to me. He was chewing on a purple carrot and eating some dark leaves. True to their name, his slender horn had a silver tint and his coat was pure white and shiny like he'd just been brushed. Of course, that wasn't the case. Despite being unable to return to the wild, none of these animals were tame.

Next to him, a grey male tried to steal some of his carrots and he grunted, chasing the cheeky thief away with a heavy nod.

"Typical Cross, always challenging The Sergeant," Nissan chuckled affectionately. "The Sergeant is the lead stallion of the herd and over there, the beautiful mare is the lead female. Her name is Sunshine."

"The silver one with the white manes?" I asked, following where she was pointing. There were a whole lot of unicorns, all varying shades of white, grey, and silver, and none of them stood very still. While I knew I'd learn to keep them apart in time, right now, they all looked the same.

The keeper nodded. "That's the one. The younger female next to her with the grey star on her forehead is Candle, their daughter. She was born here in the Sanctuary. Isn't she beautiful?"

Aaron took a step closer, having picked up on our conversation. "Did you take care of her when she was a foal?"

Nissan chuckled. "Did I? I took care of Mum all the way through her pregnancy and I was there for the birth!"

"No way. You did? I'd have loved to see her as a foal," Felicity gushed.

"What was it like?" I jumped in. I didn't usually fangirl over people but it was hard not to be amazed.

Our mentor scratched his curly beard. "Like all births. Messy, bloody, magical." He paused, waiting for a reaction like this was what most people wanted to hear but Felicity and I kept waiting for him to elaborate. "You two want to hear more, huh? Well... Sunshine had a hard pregnancy. We feared she and the baby weren't going to make it. We had another mare in the herd that challenged her and we had to separate them. When Candle was born, it took her four hours before she took her first step. That's incredibly long, in the wild, these foals need to get on their feet as quickly as possible. We were very worried that first day but everything worked out."

"Wow," Felicity sighed.

"Wow!" I echoed.

"What happened to the other mare?" Felicity scanned the herd and pointed at the third female. "Is that the one that challenged her?"

Nissan followed her gaze and chuckled. "No, no.

That's Jun-Jun, she's our old lady. She wouldn't harm a fly. No, after the birth, we didn't succeed in merging the two mares so we had to transfer the other one. It was a real shame, Thistle was wonderful. Lots of personality. That's probably why she tried to go for lead mare. But that's just the nature of things. She's leading her own herd at the Myth & Monster Conservation so it all worked out in the end."

"Oh, that's a great place. I applied there for an internship too but when I got accepted here, there was no competition," Aaron bragged, his only contribution to the conversation.

"I'm glad to hear. There are a handful

of silver blush herds in captivity, but we're one of only three places that have white-tipped antler unicorns and meadland unicorn ponies. They're a little harder to work with so that's for if you end up staying after your internship is over." Nissan scratched his cheek as he gazed over to the meadow. "I'm getting ahead of myself. Who wants to see a silver blush up close?"

All three of our hands flew up in the air.

"Eager," our mentor noted as he waved us along, bringing us closer to the meadow than any visitor could get.

From here, I had a terrific view of the herd but it was still hard to keep all the unicorns apart. I raised my hand again. "Can I take notes?"

Nissan seemed surprised but nodded. "Sure, knock yourself out."

With a grin, I grabbed the notebook from my backpack and opened it on a new page. With rough lines, I drew The Sergeant and added some arrows with notes about his appearance and characteristics. In time, I would learn all this by heart but for that to happen, I had to commit it all to memory first.

Next to me, Felicity whipped out a notebook of her own and side by side, we studied the herd. The Sergeant would be easy to recognise, he was the largest of them all and his role as lead male set him apart from the others. Same for Sunshine, she would be the one guiding the herd from the front while The Sergeant would drive it from the back.

The others would be harder to distinguish, especially the twins, but I was going to do my best. I kept my eye on the young stallion that tried to steal the carrot. He pranced back and forth, his silver coat shimmering in the sun and producing a spectacle of colours. No wonder rainbows were associated with them.

Another unicorn trotted over to The Sergeant

and the pile of purple carrots. The larger stallion huffed as soon as he spotted the youngster and chased him away with a snort. I glanced at Nissan, wondering if this was normal behaviour. While it seemed innocent enough now, if either of the two colts properly challenged the white stallion, that would cause a lot of unrest in the group.

The keeper made some notes but didn't seem worried or alarmed by their behaviour. He muttered some things under his breath and nodded. "As you might know, unicorns are very peculiar animals. They're very clever and in tune with us humans. They can have very adverse reactions to some people so we'll have to check whether they'll accept you as their keepers first," Nissan explained, waving us forward.

"How do we know if they accept us?" I questioned, glancing at the herd of silver unicorns out in the paddock.

"They won't try to kill you," he answered.

I chuckled until I realised he wasn't kidding. My laughter died out and a twinge of nerves turned my stomach into a knot. Oh.

I glanced at the other two interns to see if they were worried as well but it didn't appear so. If anything, they seemed excited.

Nissan checked his chart and nodded. "Let's go one by one. Ladies first."

"That's sexist," Aaron complained.

The keeper sighed. "Alright, gentlemen first, if the ladies don't object."

Felicity shrugged and I shook my head. I didn't care if I went first or not, if anything, sometimes it was better to have someone else go first so I knew what to expect.

Nissan opened one of the gates and the two of them stepped into the first part of the pen. The unicorns behind the fence immediately noticed Aaron and slowly, one of them set in motion. Elegantly, a large silver unicorn made his way to the fence. He sniffed the air and pressed his head against the fence, pushing a sharp horn through.

Aaron instinctively took a step back, gulping visibly.

"That's The Sergeant, our lead stallion," Nissan explained, not seeming very bothered. "He'll assess whether Aaron is acceptable or not. We're still not sure what exactly they judge people on but if you get rejected by the herd, it's lethal to try and stay."

"So if The Sergeant doesn't like me, I can't be a keeper?" I asked, suddenly worried. I'd studied and worked too hard for this, only to be rejected by a unicorn.

"Correct," Nissan replied. "He's not very interested in Aaron so that's a pass."

"Heck yeah," the other guy boasted, pumping his fist. "I'm awesome."

I gulped. If the unicorns deemed him worthy, they had interesting qualifiers.

He retreated from the pen and without checking with me, Felicity went next. Cool as a cucumber, she stepped to the fence and waited for The Sergeant to return. Almost immediately, the powerful stallion trotted back and pushed his horn through the fencing again.

Felicity remained unwavering as he stared at her. After a couple of tense seconds, he retreated and she strode out of the pen like it was nothing.

Now it was my turn.

Trembling with nerves and excitement, I made my way into the pen. The fence seemed so flimsy up close, even though I was sure it was sturdy enough.

I shuffled from side to side, waiting for the stallion to return and give me the dismissal of approval. Then I could continue chasing my dream to become an expert on mythical animals.

I waited for The Sergeant but instead of turning

back, he joined his herd and ate some hay from a suspended feeder.

What did that mean? Did this mean he was so sure I wasn't a threat that he didn't even have to see me up close?

Just when I was done waiting, another unicorn separated from the group and trotted my way. This one was more white than silver and looked a little smaller than The Sergeant.

The unicorn paused in front of the fence and stared at me with deep eyes. She nudged her horn through the fence, snorted softly, and turned away to rejoin the herd.

I released a tight breath. I passed.

"Interesting. Sunshine doesn't usually judge for the herd," Nissan muttered. "Fascinating."

"Is it bad?" I asked.

He shook his head. "No, it's just unusual. Doesn't matter, you all passed so I can officially welcome you as unicorn keepers. Well done! The real work begins tomorrow." He checked his watch and nodded. "Make sure to get a good night's sleep, you start at six."

THREE

The next morning, I woke up before sunrise so I could call Tina before I had to leave for my commute. It was painfully early but I didn't mind because I got to tell my girlfriend all about my first day.

While tucked in snuggly under my warm blankets, I dialled her number.

It only rang twice before she picked up. "Hello, hello. You've reached the girlfriend line."

My stomach fluttered when I heard her voice. "What am I supposed to press to speak to the most beautiful, adorable girlfriend?"

"Press... one," she said, attempting to mimic a robot.

"Beep, pressing one," I joked.

"Hello, this is Tina speaking," my girlfriend answered in her normal voice.

I laughed as I snuggled into my fluffy pillow. "I've been dying to talk to you."

"We've only been apart for a week."

"And it's too long. How are things over there?"

"New. I'm still settling into my new flat but I really like it here. How are things over there? How was your first day?"

"Pretty amazing. I got to see a silver blush unicorn up close. I was so close. It was the best day of my life. And to work with them, the herd had to approve of us as keepers and they did. I passed. I'm actually going to be a unicorn keeper. Can you believe it?"

"Wow, that's fantastic. I'm so proud of you. I wish I was there to celebrate."

"I know, I feel the same. I—" My phone vibrated as my second alarm went off and I got a glimpse of the time. "Ugh, I have to get going or I'm going to be late."

"That's alright. I'm just glad I heard your voice." Tina made kissy noises. "I love you. Have a great day at work."

"Love you too." Reluctantly, but not that reluctantly, I got ready to go to work. It was early but who cared? There were unicorns to be fed and checked and stables to clean.

I rushed through my morning routine and hopped on my bike. With the wind in my hair, I pedalled as fast as I could, pretending I was riding a unicorn. The Sergeant didn't look like he'd ever tolerate it but maybe under the right cirumstances, Sunshine could be convinced? Or Jun-Jun, the oldest member of the herd. In all likelihood, it would never happen but a girl could dream.

It took a good twenty minutes before the large entrance gates appeared and the sanctuary came into sight. Slightly out of breath, I parked my bike and joined the group of interns by the front. Felicity and Aaron were chatting with each other and as much as I disliked them, I didn't know anyone else.

"Morning," I greeted, giving a little wave.

"Good morning," Aaron returned politely. Apart from his sexist comment yesterday, he seemed perfectly nice.

I hoped he only parroted misogynistic things but didn't actually believe them.

Felicity looked down her nose. "You made it."

"I live to see another day," I answered, not able to keep the sarcasm out of my voice.

"We'll see about that." She turned away and

raised her arm in the direction of the approaching woman. "Good morning, Gwen! Lovely day, isn't it?"

Bootlicker.

I would've been more irritated if I didn't have a day of working at the Sanctuary ahead of me. The prospect of seeing the unicorns again excited me and I could hardly wait.

The group set in motion after the copper-haired woman and my excitement grew as we entered the Sanctuary. It was so early, the fountain hadn't even been turned on. Despite that, there were keepers and other workers around, all in uniforms or outfits with the Griffin Sanctuary's logo stitched on, finishing up whatever tasks and duties they had.

Instead of pausing at the fountain, Gwen brought us all the way to the primary staff facility in the middle of the sanctuary. The path led to a large building decorated with wooden slats and plants. I stepped inside, amazed by all the natural light coming in through the large windows. The entrance hall was clean, spacious and had nice white tiles and columns that supported the balcony on the second floor. A wolf-whistle would've been appropriate under different circumstances but my very first workday was not one of them.

Aaron and Felicity made some appreciative

comments as we followed the copper-haired woman to the dressing area. A wall of metal lockers on both sides reminded me of my old changing room at the gym or the swimming pool, except that there were a lot more and in better condition.

"You can use any free locker for your belongings and clothes. Individual changing rooms are over to the side. There are also showers and laundry bags for your uniforms."

One of the other girls raised her hand. "So we don't have to wash our own overalls?"

"Luckily not. Uniforms are kept in this cabinet. There are also sweaters, caps, jumpers, whatever you might need," Gwen responded, reaching into one of the cupboards. "There are all kinds of sizes. I need a large one myself but I like some extra room. There's a lot of lifting and bending when you work with kitsunes. They're mischievous little buggers."

"Ooh, you're a kitsune keeper?" Aaron asked from my left.

"When I find the time. I oversee all the enclosures in the left wing."

That explained that. There was a strict-ish hierarchy at a place like this and we were right at the bottom of the food chain. That was fine by me, I was grateful for the opportunity.

I waited until the others had grabbed their overalls before I grabbed a medium for myself. It was a little long so I had to roll up the legs but I needed the extra space around my waist. I put my clothes in one of the lockers and closed it up with the little key.

I caught a glimpse of myself in the mirror and a sense of pride rushed through me. There were not a lot of people who had been able to wear this uniform but I was one of them. This was real and wilder than my dreams. I was really a worker at the Griffin Sanctuary.

To top it off, Gwen handed out walkie-talkies and ID badges with our names on them. "Here are your entry passes for the gates and the service entrance. They'll give you access to all the staff facilities and you'll also need them when you're getting a meal from the cafeteria."

I eagerly accepted mine. My picture was awful but that wasn't enough to ruin my good mood. I pinned it on the front of my overalls and pulled the badge out as far as the cord allowed before letting it snap back. So official.

With my radio attached to my belt and everyone geared up, we all went to our designated zones. I wasn't looking forward to another day with Felicity and Aaron but luckily, there would be unicorns.

· · ·

WITH THE EARLY sun on my face, I enjoyed the little walk to the unicorn house. I could tell a lot of effort had been put into making the sanctuary feel as natural as possible and it really felt good.

I arrived first which gave me the chance to unlock the gate. I pulled on my badge and pressed it against the scanner, grinning as the light turned green. So freaking cool.

With my head held high, I marched into the stable, feeling a little smug that I arrived before Aaron and Felicity. Not by much, but first was first.

"I see you all made it bright and early," Nissan said from by the feeding station. He grabbed a large bucket and placed it on a set of scales. "The unicorns get fed two times a day and need a varied diet. We provide them with purple carrots and cored twin apples in the morning, which is when we do our first check of the day. There are also suspended enrichment feeders in the rest of their enclosure for hay that need refilling and water checks have to be done before the silver blushes leave the working area."

"Does every unicorn get its own portion?" Felicity questioned as she leaned in to check the scales.

"More or less. We make multiple piles to discourage fighting and keep an eye on every individual's weight." Nissan filled the bucket with the vegetables and fruits and checked the number on the scale. "There we go. Since you're all new, I'm going out into the enclosure by myself but over time, as the unicorns get used to your presence and you build a bond, you'll be able to go out into the paddock as well. We also try to feed the unicorns a carrot or two by hand so they remember where their food comes from and later, we'll have some training sessions with treats."

I pulled out my notebook and lightning-fast, wrote down everything he said. Next to me, Felicity shot me a glare and whipped out her own journal as well. The competition was on.

Nissan grabbed the heavy bucket, straining from the weight. "When I feed them, I also do our daily checks. It's important to examine their legs for any sign of limping or discomfort. Take The Sergeant, for example. Even from here, I can see he's walking without any problem so that's good. I'll have to get closer to take note of his eyes, nose, and mouth to make sure they're nice and clear. If there any discharge or discolouring, make a note of it and log it into the system. The vet checks our reports every day but if you think there's an urgent problem, there's a button to alert the vet straight away or you can use your walkie-talkie. I trust you're trained in doing these checks?"

"I am, of course." Felicity chirped immediately. "I don't know about the others though."

Aaron scoffed. "I learned this in my first year."

"I know it too," I added, not wanting to give Nissan the impression that I wasn't as qualified.

He handed us each a page and gestured to the unicorns. "Great. Prove it to me. You can each observe a unicorn and note down their conditions. I'll check it after I fed the unicorns."

I was stunned for a moment or two. I knew everyone always talked about this being a hands-on learning experience but I hadn't expected to be thrown in the deep end immediately. While it was just a routine check, this was an important part of the wellbeing of the animals. If we missed some symptoms or signs, a unicorn could really suffer for it.

Unsurprising, Aaron and Felicity immediately ran off to observe their unicorn and I only shot into action a beat behind them. I scanned the name on my form, surprised to find I was given Candle's sheet. It was clear that she was one of the pride and joys of the Sanctuary so this was an even bigger responsibility.

Nervous but excited, I scanned the white herd for the filly with the grey star on her face. She looked quite young so she was probably near her mother... Ah, there. As expected, the young unicorn was standing not too far away from Sunshine.

I moved to the side to get a better view of her. Despite being in their stables, they were still a good distance away so it wasn't super easy to get a good look at her. I kept my eyes locked on Candle, watching her every move. She scraped her hoof along the sand and sniffed one of the large leaves on the ground. With a soft nicker, she threw her head up, her beautiful white coat glistening in the sun. Her eyes were large and clear, attentive without being skittish. She looked healthy to me and I checked all the boxes. At the bottom of the sheet, there was a space for the keeper's name, the date, and my signature.

Not feeling confident that I should be filling that out, I returned to Nissan. To my surprise, Felicity and Aaron were still observing their unicorns so either I'd missed something or they weren't as skilled as they made out to be.

With a smile, I leaned against the railing,

relishing in the opportunity to look at the unicorns more. They seemed perfectly happy to have Nissan walk around their midst, eager to get the carrots from his bucket. I couldn't wait until the herd was so familiar with me that I could do that too.

After he finished, he returned to the stable to see how we did.

I handed him my sheet for Candle and looked it over, making me wait in tense silence.

This was even worse than being graded in school.

After an excruciating minute, he nodded. "Looks good, I agree with your observations. Well done, Charlotte. Oh wait, you didn't sign it."

I accepted the sheet back from him, overcome with a nervous jitter. It was one thing to note down my observations but signing it meant I suddenly became responsible for Candle's care. Terrifying.

I patted my pockets for a pen and was about to dig into my bag when Nissan held one out to me. Gratefully, I accepted it and as I jotted my name down, I saw a golden griffin with midnight wings on the end of the pen.

"I love the Sanctuary's logo," I noted, twirling the pen to make the blue wings shimmer.

Nissan smiled. "The founder herself designed it."

"I know, back when the Sanctuary was exclusively for griffins. That was over twenty years ago and now, there are almost fifty different species of mythical animals here."

An impressed look crossed my mentor's face. "You know your stuff."

"I love this place," I admitted. "I visited it all the time when I was a child."

"Then I have no doubt you'll have no trouble fitting in," Nissan supplied warmly. He gestured to the pen as I tried to hand it back. "You can keep it. From one Griffin Sanctuary fan to another."

I beamed. "Thank you."

He walked away to check with the other two interns, seeming happy with their work too. After he gathered our sheets, he made his way back into the work area to open it up so the herd could go out into the meadow. Sunshine gathered the herd while The Sergeant encouraged them forward, out of the sandy grove and towards the grassy plains. I wished I could've spent more time with them but my desires were irrelevant to the rhythm of the group. There was a fine balance between taking good care of the animals and letting nature do its thing. Too much interference would modify how they behaved and render any discoveries about the species useless. The more we learned about their instincts and natural way of things, the more the research would be able to help protect their wild cousins. In the case of the silver blush unicorns, there weren't that many left so anything we discovered could help change that.

With a deep breath, I centred myself as the herd disappeared behind some bushes. I knew this wasn't the last time I would see them but I still felt sad that my first encounter with the unicorns was over. Hopefully, I'd see them again soon.

Nissan dusted off his hands as he finished with his notes. "That's it for today. I hope you enjoyed your first taste of being a keeper."

"Loved it!" Felicity chimed as she fluttered her eyelashes at him.

"You all did a good job. That's the fun part of the day. Now who is ready to get their hands dirty?"

Eagerly, all three of us agreed.

A little taken aback by our enthusiasm, the bearded keeper chuckled. "Alright, follow me." He led us towards the right side and pushed the sliding barn door to the side, giving us access to the communal stall. The straw was all trampled from the sleeping horses and big heaps of poop were scattered throughout.

"I think this is pretty self-explanatory," Nissan grinned, looking pretty pleased with himself. "There are pitchforks and shovels over here and you'll find fresh straw and hay in the shed. I have to log the notes and check something with Gwen, can I leave you to it?"

Another collective nod from the three of us reassured him and he went on his merry way, probably under the impression that we got along and made an excellent team. He'd barely closed the door or Aaron had something to say.

He gestured to the shed and the wheelbarrow parked outside. "It takes a pretty strong person to move those so I'll do that while you little ladies shovel shit."

My mouth fell slightly aghast. What an arrogant prick. From all my years as a student, I'd met plenty of types like him. People who thought they were God's gift and it looked like nice-guy Aaron was one of them. Great...

"Ass," Felicity muttered under her breath.

First thing we agreed on.

With a big smile, I grabbed one of the shovels and threw it towards him. "Don't you worry about us little ladies, we're all perfectly qualified," I said with my sweetest smile.

Felicity laughed and it took her a mere second to catch up with me. "Airhead over here is right. Why don't you step into modern times and educate yourself on gender equality? We can all take turns shovelling shit."

If I was the type to snap my fingers sassily, this would have been the moment. Except that wasn't me at all, so I just kept smiling while Aaron's head turned red. Looked like he wasn't used to being called out on his sexism.

Triumphantly, I grabbed the pitchfork and made my way into the stable to shovel poop with as much dignity as I could muster. Felicity made her way to the shed and to my surprise, Aaron put his shovel to good use. Despite the initial hick-up, we worked in relative silence and cleaned out the unicorn enclosure without any complaining or bickering. I supposed we were all too proud for that. For three people as different as night and day, we sure had some annoying similarities.

Besides, we always knew this was part of the job so what was one more day of shit-duty?

The inside of my hands were burning from the repeated shovelling but I kept smiling through the discomfort. My palms would harden soon enough and I'd get used to the smell.

I glanced at the other two, trying to figure out if they were suffering as much as I did. To my annoyance, Aaron's bulging muscles suggested otherwise and Felicity looked strangely comfortable pushing the wheelbarrow around.

Stubbornly, I focused my attention back on the task at hand. The unicorn poop was quite different from horse droppings. Rounder and not quite as... splatty. I had to guess that was a result of the multiple stomachs they had.

"Looks like we're almost done," Felicity announced from the full wheelbarrow.

She had surprised me. She looked all girly and delicate, but there was a hard worker underneath the stuck-up shell that wasn't above little jobs like this.

I wiped the sweat off my forehead. "That didn't take us that long."

"Yeah, we did a banging job," Aaron added, resting his foot on the shovel.

Felicity clicked her tongue. "Not bad for two little ladies, huh?"

I released a full belly laugh and the other two stared at me for a second before joining in. Our laughter filled the stable as we wheeled the waste away and finished up the job. Strange how different people could bond so easily over menial labour.

In a much more amicable mood than how we came here, we let Nissan know we were done and his appraising nod after he checked the stables had me soaring the whole walk back to the wishing fountain.

"Guess we should get going," Felicity remarked, albeit reluctantly.

"At least it's an early start tomorrow," I said, looking forward to being here. I didn't even mind waking up before dawn.

Aaron shrugged. "We'll get used to it. Which campus are you on?"

"B," Felicity replied.

"Same," he said, turning to me. "You?"

Stunned, I blinked slowly. "What campus?"

"The off-site campus with dormitories for the interns and workers," Felicity clarified. "Did your school not arrange for you to stay there?"

I frowned. "No."

"Shame," she commented, not sounding like she meant it. "Oh, well. See you tomorrow then."

She and Aaron made their way to the exit, leaving me annoyed and blindsided. If there was accommodation available for students like us, why had nobody informed me about that?

FOUR

The first week at the Griffin Sanctuary flew by. There was so much to do, I was barely keeping up. While there were a lot of routine tasks involved in caring for the unicorns, every day was different. Slowly but surely, I was getting to know the individual personalities of the herd and it only confirmed what I already knew. I loved unicorns.

It had been a challenge keeping up with the long hours and hard work but after visiting admin, my school had approved the move to the off-campus dormitory and I got to move out of my little studio.

Criminally early, I hauled my luggage off the shuttle bus and rolled it towards the cluster of buildings. With a couple of shops and a gym, it was more a small village than a campus. It had everything workers living away from home needed.

Pausing in front of the building, I checked my information sheet for the entrance code and entered block B. The hallway smelled of cleaning products, a great sign, and the small but functional elevator took me up to the third floor. The rooms here were just sleeping quarters with a communal kitchen, bathroom, and living areas, but that was fine by me. Hopefully, I'd be able to socialise with some other people besides Felicity and Aaron.

My luggage rattled as I pulled it along the smooth floor, counting the numbers on the doors until I found mine. I pressed my badge against the scanner and with a soft click, the door unlocked.

I pushed into the room, pleasantly surprised. It was small, but there was a double bed and a large window that invited a lot of light into the space. The sheets looked crisp and there was a small wardrobe with a couple of lone coathangers on a rail. Neat, not any worse than my studio, and I didn't have to pay for it.

"Welcome to the building," a sharp, slightly sarcastic voice said from behind me.

I turned around, not surprised to see Felicity standing in the doorframe.

"Thanks..." I replied in the same tone, not sure what she was doing here. I glanced over her shoulder, spotting the open door of the room across. I rolled my eyes. "Let me guess, your room is across the hall."

"Aren't you perceptive?"

Not in the mood to deal with Felicity, I waved her out of the room and closed the door. That was a minus point of living here but it wasn't the building's fault that she was such a pain. And our internship was only six months so hopefully, I didn't have to put up with her for longer than that. If I got chosen to stay.

A quick look at my watch confirmed I didn't have time to unpack my suitcase. There were unicorns that needed tending and they didn't wait for anyone.

After barely spending five minutes in my new room, I was already back on the road. Nissan didn't appreciate tardiness and frankly, I didn't want to miss a minute of unicorn time.

In little to no time, I arrived at the Sanctuary staff entrance. It wasn't as grand as entering through the beautiful front gates but it felt so official. I had to show my ID badge and got access to all the backstage areas, which were arguably much more interesting than the public areas.

I changed in the locker room and dressed in a fresh and crisp uniform, I made my way over to the unicorn house. To my dismay, Aaron and Felicity were already there and even though I was more than on time, they made me look late. Annoying.

Tomorrow, I would set off even earlier.

Nissan arrived only mere minutes later, looking pleasantly surprised that we were all there. "Good morning."

"Morning," I chimed in sync with the other two. I really had my work cut out for me with this kind of competition. It would take a lot more than my usual tactics to show that I was the best.

"Let's get started," our mentor said. He put his green work boots on and waved us into the stable, whistling a soft tune. "I think today, I'll let you come into the working area with me."

I held back a squeal. "We get to go into the enclosure?"

"Yeah, why not. We'll work together. I'll feed the unicorns and you three can do the health checks. As a full-time keeper, this is one of the most important things you'll have to do. If you build a good rapport with your animals, it'll be easier to carry out these checks." He walked over to the breakfast area where we weighed out the food. Luckily, the unicorns loved carrots and twin apples, which kept for a long time without spoiling.

Nissan showed us how to portion the unicorn's breakfast and with the buckets filled, we made our way to the enclosure. He pulled the lever to open the unicorn's stable and out they came. One by one and rather slowly, the herd mosied their way into the sandy work area.

"Before we enter, we always make sure to check the mood of our animals. Their body language is much easier to read than ours and they're much more reactive too. Don't make the mistake of thinking they won't attack you because they didn't yesterday." Nissan observed the unicorns for a couple of minutes before nodding. "Okay, you can tell they're relaxed. Sunshine is in an amicable mood and The Sergeant is patiently putting up with Criss and Cross. That's always a good sign. Let's go in."

I could barely contain my excitement. I was going to be within arms reach of a unicorn. I'd be standing so close, I could touch one. This was insane.

The three of us followed Nissan into the work area. While it was incredibly exhilarating to be in here, it was also terrifying. Just like our mentor said, these animals were wild and wouldn't hesitate to attack us if they panicked or perceived us as a threat.

I wiped my sweaty palms on my uniform, trying to keep calm. Any loud noises or abrupt movements could startle the herd and that would not be good.

While Nissan put out the breakfast and talked to the herd in a cheerful and friendly voice, we divided the log sheets. There were six unicorns and three of us, so we each got to assess two of them.

I sought out the two unicorns I was supposed to check, easily spotting The Sergeant near the largest pile of food. He looked relaxed and calm as he chewed on the purple roots, his silver coat a little ruffled from a night's sleep. Once he was finished with his pile, he moved to another heap, chasing Cross away. The young colt nickered softly but had no choice to step out of the way. Smart, considering The Sergeant's status and power. He moved with grace but he was an absolute unit with large hooves and a thick horn that could do some serious damage.

He looked in great health so I marked that down and moved onto my assessment of Candle, his daughter. Just like yesterday, she was glued to Sunshine's side. She followed her mother around, gently nibbling on some of the apples. She gave a longing look at the pile of carrots her father was eating but The Sergeant didn't look like he was sharing with anyone. Both of them looked healthy and happy.

With my two unicorns checked out, I glanced at the other members of the herd. The energetic twins were bouncing and ready to go out into the meadow. It was always a joy to watch the colts play with each other. Cross chased after his brother and in the process, bumped into the elderly Jun-Jun.

She whinnied a warning as she stepped away. There was the slightest tremble in her step but I wasn't sure if that was from being spooked or something else. She was eating well and interacting with the other unicorns in the group, so no real signs of pain or distress. Maybe it was nothing... Besides, I wasn't even meant to be watching her. Surely, if it was worth mentioning, Felicity would do when she briefed Nissan.

We gathered to give our mentor our findings and I listened closely when Felicity was going over Jun-Jun's checklist. I agreed with all her observations but there was no mention of her limp.

Should I say something? I could be making it up and it would reflect badly on the other intern if I went over her head. But leg injuries were particularly bad for unicorns, often being fatal. If I could prevent a lot of pain and suffering for Jun-Jun, wasn't it important that I spoke up?

I glanced at the unicorn out in the working area. She seemed to be walking fine but it was hard to tell from this far.

It was probably nothing...

No. I couldn't let my worries of stepping on someone's toes influence my care for these animals. I had to say something. It was better to be wrong than neglectful.

Awkwardly, I raised my hand.

Felicity stopped talking and shot me a glare while Aaron snickered that I was raising my hand. Nissan turned to me. "Yes?"

"I don't mean to butt in but... I think I saw Jun-Jun slightly limping."

"Why were you watching my unicorn?" Felicity questioned sharply.

Nissan ignored her question and made his way to the fence to observe the herd. He watched the silver blush trot around the sandy work area in search of more food. Her back leg twitched slightly, barely noticeable if we hadn't been paying attention.

"You're right," Nissan concluded. "Limps can quickly become a real detriment to unicorns so we'll isolate her and call the vet to check her out," he added as he swiped his finger over the tablet. "Well-spotted."

A sense of pride rolled over me. I wasn't going crazy and it was good that I spoke up. Even if I could feel Felicity shooting daggers with her eyes. It wasn't my fault that she hadn't noticed it.

Nissan grabbed another carrot out of the bucket. "Jun-Jun is usually very good with her recall training so let's see if she wants to come in."

We made our way over to the stables where he pulled a lever to open it back up. All three of us followed and watched him closely as he whistled his fingers to get the mare's attention.

"Jun-Jun. Come here, girl!" he shouted, waving her over.

The elderly unicorn hesitated a little and scraped one of her front legs over the ground.

"Come on, Jun!" Nissan tried again, gaining the attention of one of the young males.

Criss? Or Cross? It was hard to keep the twins apart.

The colt mosied towards the stable, his ears flicking back and forth in curiosity. He paused in front of the metal bars and snorted softly, his eyes fixated on the carrot in Nissan's hand.

"I didn't call you, Cross," Nissan chuckled,

moving the carrot away. "You're always so cheeky. Can't resist getting a bit of attention, huh? Go on, big boy. I'm trying to get Junbug in here."

The unicorn flicked his ears and moved away in the slowest fashion possible. It was like he understood he wasn't wanted and reacted like a stroppy teenager.

I held back a smile. It was clear all the unicorns had their own little personality and I couldn't wait to get to know them.

"Juuuuun, come here, you big girl!" Nissan tried again, whistling to gain the silver's attention.

After a moment or two, the beautiful unicorn set in motion and the faint morning sun made her silver coat shimmer as she mosied over to us. Despite her age, she was still a sight to behold. Her muscles moved visibly under her skin with every step as she entered the stable.

Nissan pulled the lever again to close the door behind her and offered her the carrot. "Good girl. Now let's have a good look at you, see what's going on with your leg."

Excited to get to witness a unicorn up close, I moved towards the stable, fighting for my place between Aaron and Felicity.

"You're crowding me," she hissed, trying to push me back with her elbow.

"I can't see," I muttered as I tried to look over her shoulder.

"You little ladies need to stop being so catty," Aaron weighed in.

We both snapped around and glared at him.

"Shut up, Aaron," Felicity sneered.

"Yes, shut up," I backed her up.

"Ahem." Nissan cleared his throat at our squabbling and shook his head. "I appreciate that you're all eager to help, but if you can't work together, I have no need for you. Understood?"

Embarrassed, I lowered my head. "Sorry."

Felicity and Aaron mumbled apologies of their own as we gave each other some space. I knew our infighting was petty and childish but we all knew that our performance as interns would influence whether we could get a full-time job here. Working at a sanctuary like this with mythical animals was a dream come true for most of us so having to be nice to my competition, knowing they could shatter my dream, wasn't easy. But Nissan was right. We were here to do one job, and that was to take care of the animals, not be ruled by our emotions. They didn't understand if we had a bad day or if we didn't like our colleagues. We had to be consistent, dedicated, always putting their needs first.

Nissan fed Jun-Jun a purple carrot as a reward for coming in. While she ate the treat, it gave us the perfect opportunity to get a good look at her. She shifted her weight and it became clear that she was avoiding using her left hind leg.

"Oof, that's not good," Nissan muttered. "I think we'll have to call the vet. I hope we don't have to put her under though.

"Of course. Lots of large animals, like unicorns, react badly to anaesthetic," I quipped in. "There's a real chance she wouldn't wake up from it."

"Exactly," Nissan said, his tone appreciative. "I'm impressed you know that."

"I knew that too," Felicity interjected.

I ignored her. "Maybe it's just an abscess?" I theorised. "The weather has been all over the place so sometimes, that leads to infections."

"It's hard to tell." Nissan reached for his walkie-talkie and brought it to his mouth. "Nissan for Jacob."

After some static noise, the crackling stopped. "This is Jacob. What can I do for you?"

"Hey. I was hoping you had some time to pop by the silver blush unicorns. Our Jun-Jun has a bit of a limp. I'm hoping it's nothing but I don't want to send her out in the meadow like this."

"Understood. Let me check my schedule," Jacob answered. The radio clicked. "Alright, I'll make some time. I'll be there in... fifteen?"

"Thanks, man." Nissan hooked his walkie-talkie back onto his belt and sighed. "Alright, I'm going to move the rest of the herd out before they get too curious. You wait here for the vet."

Muttering, he made his way out of the stable, leaving the three of us with Jun-Jun.

"She's really pretty up close," I noted, staring up at the beautiful unicorn. With silver manes cascading down her neck and the long elegant horn, she was truly elegant and graceful. She moved around in the pen, occasionally bumping against the sides. The loud clangs and shaking fence really illustrated her immense power and I wondered how the vet would check her leg without having to subdue her.

"You're such a teacher's pet," Felicity grumbled as she tried to get a better look of Jun-Jun. "This was my unicorn to check. You should've told me instead of upstaging me."

"It's not my fault you missed her limp," I countered, holding back the urge to apologise. This was a very competitive field and if the roles were reversed, I was sure Felicity would've jumped on the chance to make me look bad too. That being said, it didn't feel great stepping on her on the way up. Next time, I'd handle it differently.

With a dismissive scoff, the other girl turned away so she could ignore me. Aaron wasn't dumb enough to insert himself into our argument so we waited in silence for the vet. The tension made the fifteen minutes feel like fifteen hours but eventually, Nissan returned to the stable with a dark middle-aged man by his side.

"Let's see what we have," Jacob said in a deep voice. He put his briefcase down next to a bale of straw and glanced into the pen. He observed Jun-Jun for a bit, watching her pace up and down in search of more carrots. With a knowing hum, Jacob reached into his white coat and pulled out a notepad. "It's hard to tell without getting a closer look at that hoof. At her age, I'm not comfortable giving Jun-Jun an anaesthetic. There's too much risk that she won't wake up."

I felt Felicity and Aaron glance at me as the vet said exactly what I had earlier. Pride filled my chest as I called it correctly and made me feel a little better about myself and my education. I wasn't attending

Evergreen University like Aaron, or whatever all-star school Felicity went to, but I'd been paying attention in my classes.

Jacob took his off coat and rolled up his sleeves. "I wouldn't do this with just any unicorn but I've been treating Jun-Jun since she came to the Sanctuary five years ago. Let's see if she'll let us take a look." He reached for the metal bar that opened the pen and pulled it to the side just enough that he and Nissan could pass through.

The two men worked together to get Jun-Jun in position, with one of them asking her to present her hoof on a little step while the other rewarded her with chunks of carrot.

"I thought perhaps it was an abscess," I voiced again, earning more glares from my peers. I knew I wasn't making myself very popular but I'd rather impress the vet than the other two interns.

"That would be on my list of first guesses," Jacob remarked, managing to lift up Jun-Jun's leg enough to get a look at the underside of the hoof. "Let's see, let's see. There it is. It is an abscess. And a nasty one at that, but superficial. I should be able to drain it. Ah, I left my briefcase. Can one of you open it and get out the hoof knife?"

Eagerly, all three of us jumped on the case and

rummaged through the contents, all hoping to be the first one to find it.

"Got it!" Aaron cheered as he got his hands first on the knife with the curve at the end. He rushed to the pen and handed it through the bars to the vet, looking pretty pleased with himself.

Fierce competition, indeed.

There was no doubt I'd have to stay on the ball with these two vying just as much for the same position. But I wasn't scared of a fight and I never backed down when it came to animals.

The entire day, we tried to upstage each other in an endless competition to see who was the best. There was no doubt that Felicity and Aaron were worthy rivals and after a long day, I was glad to be back at the dorm.

Exhausted from the constant pressure, I flopped on my bed and I scrolled through my contact list for my girlfriend's name. I should unpack and make my room homey but that could wait. Talking to Tina was much more important.

My chest fluttered as I held my phone against my ear, waiting for the call to go through.

A warm voice came through the speaker. "Hey hey."

"Hi." I turned on my stomach, trying to get comfortable. "It's so good to hear your voice."

Tina chuckled. "You heard my voice yesterday."

"And I missed you every moment since. I wish you were here."

She laughed softly. "You're still not getting along with the other interns?"

I groaned. "No. Felicity and Aaron are the worst. And guess who lives across the hall?"

"Who?"

"Felicity. Of course, it's Felicity." I pretended to gag. "I really want a break from her smug face."

"You're so salty," Tina teased.

"I know." I adjusted my pillow and rolled on my back. "How are things over there?"

"Pretty good. I'm getting along with the other students just fine. The people here are really nice. There's even a girl here from Evergreen University."

"Aaron is from Evergreen too. He's so arrogant. If they're all like that, I'm glad I didn't get in."

Tina snorted. "I don't know about all of them. Rebecca is super nice."

"Lucky."

"So are you settling in well? Is your room nice?"

"I'd be much nicer with you in it," I purred.

"Cute. I'll see if I can come visit on my next day off. Or you could come over here?"

I got off the bed so I could pace up and down. "I'd like that. I'm not sure when I'll have a day off though."

"Same." Tina was silent for a bit. "It'll be fine. Six months isn't that long anyway. Right?"

"Right. Lots of couples do long distance for much longer than that." I paused in front of the window, basking in the warmth of the setting sun. The gentle heat made me yawn and I rotated my arm. "I'm tired."

"You should go to bed."

"I will, I just wanted to talk to you. I miss you."

"I miss you too."

I grinned from ear to ear. "I can't wait to see you again."

"Me too. I love you."

"I love you too." I tried to stifle another yawn but it broke free anyway.

Tina's warm voice came through the speaker. "Go to sleep. We'll talk more soon."

I nodded, only realising how tired I was when I sat back down on the bed. "Talk soon. Bye, T. Sleep well."

"Sweet dreams, Char."

The line clicked as she hung up and with a grin, I got in bed. I hugged my pillow, wishing it was my girlfriend, and sank in a deep sleep with dreams about Tina and unicorns.

FIVE

One of the things I still needed to get used to was the communal aspect of shared living. The kitchen was buzzing with the other interns, some of whom I didn't even recognise. A couple of girls were grouped around the island but most of the people seemed to be having quick breakfast on their own. At least I felt better about not being the only one that just managed a bowl of cereal.

I spotted Aaron on the couch with a girl I didn't know, but no Felicity. Nice. That meant I could eat my breakfast in peace. Life was better without Miss Perfect and her know-it-all attitude.

Within seconds, I devoured my cereal and got going for our first morning meeting. They held them every day but the interns hadn't been invited until now. I supposed the Sanctuary was getting used to us as much as we were getting used to being here.

Excited for the briefing, I rushed through my morning routine and jumped on the shuttle bus with the other interns. So much handier than getting on my bike.

There was light chatter on the bus between some of the groups, but I kept to myself. Making friends wasn't my strength plus, I didn't come here to make friends. That would just make it harder when some of us got eliminated out of the process. This way, there were no hard feelings. At least, not for me.

I followed along with the group to the primary staff facility to get changed. The locker room was full and there was a slight wait to use one of the private changing rooms. I wasn't super shy so I just put on my overall in front of everyone. It wasn't like anyone was watching, everyone was too busy strapping on their walkie-talkies and gearing up for the day.

Dressed for the job, I made my way over to the staff room where the morning meeting was taking place and joined Aaron and Nissan. The other interns also surrounded their head-keeper as we waited for Gwen to start the meeting.

Unsure, I glanced at the door. No Felicity yet. What was she doing? Had she already given up?

That would be good, that meant less competition for me.

After a couple of minutes everyone had found their place in the small staff room. It was clear that it wasn't made for all of us, which explained why the interns weren't here to cramp up the meeting every day.

Right as we were getting started, Felicity hurried in and took place behind Nissan. She was a bit dishevelled for her usually neat appearance and looked slightly out of it. I wanted to ask what that was about but that involved talking to Felicity, so I kept to myself.

"Morning, everyone," Gwen said as she took place at the head of the table. "Let's go over yester-day's events and today's agenda. Maia, griffins first."

A petite woman with dark hair flicked her notes. "Right, everything is going well in the griffin house. Leia is recovering from her surgery and Cece is due any day now."

A wave of excited chatter passed through the group.

"Griffin cubs?"

"Awww!"

"Finally!"

I grinned. Griffin cubs were super exciting, I

hoped I'd still be around when they were born so I could see them. They were so endangered, it was rare to see one in real life, let alone little cubs.

Gwen seemed pleased. "That's fantastic news. We'll put preparations for the birthing suite on the agenda. Okay, unicorns next."

"Everything's going well," Nissan responded. "Thanks to my intern, we discovered Jun-Jun had an abscess in one of her hooves, but Jacob's been monitoring it and he's confident it's cleared right up."

Even though he didn't name me, I felt a wave of pride wash over me. It was still really amazing that he acknowledged my contribution. Hopefully, my attentiveness would help me secure a permanent job here.

"That's a relief," Gwen responded. She flicked through one of her notes and held out a file. "We've been in contact with the reserve on the Dwensel Plains and they're sending us a young, rescued colt. They're hoping we can fit him in with our herd. Here are the details, I'll leave the preparations to you."

Nissan accepted the file and flicked through it. "Great, we'll get started right away."

He got up and beckoned for us to follow. I wanted to hear more about the updates in the rest of the Sanctuary but I also didn't want to miss out on the arrival of a new unicorn. It sounded exciting but also tragic. There were only a handful of reasons why a wild unicorn would be brought into captivity and almost all of them were due to poachers or loss of habitat. In an ideal world, there would be no unicorns in captivity because they weren't endangered.

Despite only having worked at the Sanctuary for a short time, I felt a real sense of home when we arrived at the unicorn enclosure. I could smell the hay, the animals, hear the soft scraping of hooves on the bedding. The familiar sounds made my heart flutter, knowing I got to see the unicorns again.

The sliding door shrieked as Nissan pulled it open and we stepped into the stable. By now, I had my own wellies waiting by the entrance and I quickly put them on so we could approach the silver blushes.

"Right." Nissan rubbed his hands together. "We're dividing tasks today. Two of you should check the habitat and do breakfast while I'm going to prepare an area in the quarantine bay for our newcomer. Who wants to help me?"

"Me!" Aaron exclaimed.

"Me," I responded a second later, glancing at

Felicity. How were we going to decide who got to help Nissan?

To my surprise, Felicity just shrugged, her gaze absent. "I'll stay."

Why wasn't she fighting to work with Nissan instead of grunt duty? What was going on with her? This was nothing like the pushy, overachiever I'd been competing with.

"Eager," Nissan commented, not noticing the difference. "We'll do turns. Aaron, you can join me first."

Bah, that meant I was stuck with grumpy-Felicity. I didn't know what was going on with her but there was no way this version of her could be any more tolerable than her usual form.

With the boys gone, it would make sense to divide tasks again.

"Want to check the enclosure or do breakfast?" I asked, not having a preference.

Felicity shrugged. "I don't mind."

So weird...

"I'll do the habitat," I suggested, deciding that it would be less detrimental if she made a mistake in her apathetic state while weighing carrots than making sure the paddock was safe. If she missed a gap in the fence, that could be a disaster while a couple of extra vegetables wouldn't be an issue.

I opened the metal gate and stepped into the working area where we fed the animals. It was surrounded by a nice stone wall and led out into a field with a bit of grass, some more sand, and a small watering hole. There were a couple of wonky trees to provide shade with elevated feeders that we had to fill with hay.

It was a short walk along the perimeter and when I was confident that the fences were all in good shape and the wind hadn't blown in any trash, I returned to the working area where Felicity had piled up the carrots and apples for the unicorns.

I could hear their impatient hoof-scraping and snorting from the stable, a sign they were ready to come out and have their breakfast. I shouldn't have been surprised that even depressed Felicity was competent.

"Ready to let the unicorns out?" I asked.

She nodded. "Yeah, let's do it."

Excited, I pulled the lever that controlled the hatch. As soon as the unicorns heard the metal scraping, they set in motion and emerged from the stable. Sunshine came out first and neighed softly, raising her head up to the sun. A rainbow of colours danced along her silver coat as she stepped out into the open. The rest of the herd followed her, making a beeline for the food on the floor.

At first sight, everyone looked happy and healthy. I grabbed the clipboard to fill out our observations and handed Felicity half of the sheets. She accepted them and we checked the unicorns in silence.

It was a little weird working with her without snarky comments or condescending suggestions on how I could do better, but I enjoyed the silence. This was the first time that we did the assessment entirely on our own and I didn't want to mess it up.

SIX

Since we weren't allowed to go into the enclosure with the unicorns yet, we opened the gate to the rest of the habitat and let them leave on their own accord. Sunshine expertly got the herd's attention and with a whinny, she encouraged them out into the meadow where they would graze for the rest of the day. Maybe have the occasional lick of a salt block.

Candle followed obediently while Cross tried to take a playful bite out of his twin's behind. The two colts darted off, bouncing with energy while Jun-Jun seemed a little sleepy still. With The Sergeant guarding their back, the herd ventured out into the meadow, leaving some delightful presents for us to clean up.

"Great," I muttered, glancing at Felicity for any

action or reaction. It was weird seeing her without initiative and her take-charge attitude. Something was definitely up and as annoying as I found her, I liked this even less.

I grabbed a pitchfork and shovel, holding the latter out to her. "Are you okay?"

"Hmm?" She jolted out of her thoughts and nodded. "What?"

"Are you alright? You don't seem too good."

"I'm fine," she responded, snatching the shovel from my hand. "Let's just get to work."

There was a trace of her usual snarkiness and annoyance but it lacked the usual snark and wit. I wanted to point that out to her but then what did I know? We'd only known each other for two weeks and it wasn't like we were friends. If she wanted to be like this, whatever. I'd asked if she was okay so if she didn't want to elaborate, that was her prerogative.

"Want the stable or the working area? I don't mind the stable," I said, a last attempt to be considerate. It was less stuffy outside so maybe some fresh air would get her head sorted out.

Felicity shrugged as she made her way into the enclosure, not even bothering to reply.

"Alright then, be that way," I muttered under my breath, making my way into the stable to shovel shit.

As expected from a group of six sizable unicorns, there was a good amount of poop spread around the floor and most of the straw was trampled and crushed. It would be hard work to clean this out by myself but that was just part of the job.

I put some gloves on and scooped the piles of poop into the wheelbarrow first. Scoop after scoop, I worked my way through the stable. With a sigh, I put the pitchfork to the side and pushed the wheelbarrow out. My arms twinged and quivered from the effort, not quite used to the daily labour yet. It was a lot different compared to sitting behind desks and listening to lecturers.

As I rolled past the paddock, I looked in to see how Felicity was doing and froze. The other girl was lying on the ground, lucky to have missed the heap of shit next to her.

With a thud, I dropped the wheelbarrow and rushed towards the working area, crouching down next to her. "Hey, can you hear me?"

No reaction.

I softly slapped her cheeks. Under different circumstances, a dream come true, but right now, a real cause for worry. "Felicity. Can you hear me?"

Nothing. That wasn't good. Oh no, oh no, oh no.

A hit of panic washed over me as I tried to pull

my gloves off, wrestling with the fabric. Why did they make them so tight?

"Come on, you stupid— Finally." I pulled the gloves off and pressed my index and middle finger against Felicity's neck. It took a moment to calm myself down enough to actually register the pulse and I relaxed slightly. A heartbeat was good, at least she wasn't dead. I couldn't imagine my colleague and known rival dying on my watch would be good for my reputation.

I pushed her chin up and brought my ear to her mouth, checking for breathing.

"W-What are you doing?" her faint voice sneered in my ear.

I snapped up, overwhelmed with a huge sense of relief. "You're awake."

"What's going on?" Felicity pushed herself up from the sandy ground, the confusion written on her face.

"I don't know, I found you on the ground."

"I must've fainted." She rubbed her forehead and groaned. "Oh, I don't feel so good."

I held back the urge to remind her I'd told her so and instead, helped her up. She leaned heavily on me as we paced back to the stable, her arm around my shoulders for support. From the corners of my eyes, I could see the herd happily grazing in the meadow, oblivious to what was going on here. At least we didn't have to worry about a group of ferocious predators stalking us.

I set her down on the floor, wafting some fresh air into her face.

"Stop that," she huffed, trying to swat my hand away. "I'm fine."

"I don't think so. I'm going to get a medic over here." I reached for my radio, but she stopped me.

"I said I'm fine. Let's just get back to work."

"No way. You need to see a doctor or something."

She pushed me away and got up, swaying, barely able to stand upright. "I just had a bad night's sleep and the sun was a little brighter than expected."

I wasn't sure why she was being so stubborn, then again, I didn't really know her very well. I wanted to insist she needed medical attention but I wasn't her mother. She was a grown woman, she could take care of herself. Although the evidence was kind of proving otherwise, I wasn't going to force her to see a doctor.

"It's your decision." I shrugged, returning to the wheelbarrow. "But if you're doing it because you don't want to miss a moment with the animals, you're being stupid. They deserve keepers that are healthy and well to take care of them. Not someone who can barely stand up."

Surprisingly, that got through to Felicity. She growled but retreated. "Fine, I'll go to the medical office but you better not use this to get ahead or I'll smother you in your sleep."

I smiled. That was more like it. "I'd like to see you try."

With Felicity gone, I used my radio to let Nissan know I was manning the stable on my own and continued clearing out the straw. A lovely breeze came in through the metal bars and played with my hair as I prepared the stable for the next night.

Focused on getting my wheelbarrow of trampled straw to the waste pile, I almost bumped into a small group of people.

"Woops," a middle-aged woman chuckled, jumping out of the way.

"Sorry," I quickly said before realising I didn't recognise them. They weren't wearing uniforms either so what were they doing over here? "Umm... excuse me, but this is a staff-only zone."

The woman smiled and pulled a worker's badge from her pocket. "You must be new. I'm Starlise—"

My eyes widened as I figured out why the

woman looked familiar. "Director Starlise? I'm so sorry, I didn't recognise you."

"No worries, you were hard at work."

My cheeks were burning from my mistake. I couldn't believe I'd just told the founder, director, and owner of the Sanctuary, that this was a staff-only zone. How embarrassing. At least I was alone here so nobody else had witnessed it, well, except for her two guests.

To make sure I didn't make the same mistake, I scanned both their faces. The teenage girl looked somewhat like the director but I didn't recognise the middle-aged man.

Director Starlise noticed me staring and gestured to the two people. "This is my brother-in-law, Mark, and my niece, Reya. I'm just giving them a tour of the Sanctuary. Have the unicorns left already?"

"Yes, they're out in the paddock," I responded, gesturing to the field where the unicorns were nipping at some of the higher hay in the feeders.

The man seemed excited. "I love unicorns. Shall we have a look, Reya?"

The girl rolled her eyes. "Unicorns are dumb."

Her words stabbed me in the heart. How could she say that? And she was Starlise's niece? The amazing woman that started the Griffin Sanctuary to save lots of animals? How were they related?

Unfazed by her stroppy response, Reya's father shrugged. "Suit yourself. I'm going to have a closer look."

"This way," Starlise said as they went into the stable. Before she left, she gestured to her niece. "Oh, if you need some help, put Reya to work. She could use a bit of exercise."

With the adults gone, I joined the boss's niece at the fence. "Hi."

Engrossed on her phone, the teenager didn't even look up.

"I'm Charlotte, I'm an intern." I hesitated, not sure if I should ask her to help or not. Director Starlise had said to put her to work but she didn't look interested. "Do you want to help with the stables?

That earned me a first look from her. Well. Glare.

"Do I look like I'm dressed to shovel shit?" she snapped.

And this was why I didn't like teenagers. They were always so sassy. I looked the girl up and down, and arguably, her pinkish dress, open-toed sandals, and bracelets weren't the most practical.

I shrugged. "If that's the problem, there are extra overalls in the staff room."

Reya shot me a disgusted look. "You must be insane if you think I'd wear..." she pointed at me. "That. It's so unfashionable."

"So you're not going to help?"

She snapped her fingers. "Correct."

"Wow. Just wow." I couldn't believe my ears. Working at this Sanctuary was a dream come true and I'd put in a lot of effort to get here. How could someone related to the owners not take advantage of that opportunity? What an absolute waste.

"Suit yourself." Not wanting to argue with Reya anymore, I grabbed the empty wheelbarrow and used my frustration to push it along the sandy path. If she was too sour to appreciate the majesty of the unicorns, that was her loss. I wasn't going to let her spoil my day.

SEVEN

Exhausted from a long day doing all the work at the unicorn enclosure, I returned to the dorms with an aching back and tensed muscles. I was in desperate need of a hot shower and some food to refuel all the energy I'd used.

I arrived at the dorm and took the elevator up to the intern floor. We were all on different schedules so the living area was mostly abandoned, apart from a rather pathetic figure sitting at the island.

I paused opposite Felicity, unsure whether to strike up a conversation or not. I didn't really care about her but that didn't mean I enjoyed watching her suffer.

"Hey," I said eventually.

She looked up from her tablet, her long blonde hair cascading down her face instead of tied up. "Hi."

"How are you feeling?"

Felicity shrugged. "Ehh."

I waited to see if she had more to say but after a couple of moments of silence, nothing followed. I drummed my hands on the island and got up to make myself a cup of tea, glad I had something to do to break the awkward silence. I felt bad for Felicity, even though I wasn't sure why. It wasn't like I cared about her. If anything, her being off her game was good for me. If she wasn't performing well, then there was more chance that they'd offer me a permanent position.

But there was also something satisfactory about beating a worthy rival. I wasn't the kind of person to kick someone when they were down. Being better than Felicity when she was such a miserable mess was hardly brag-worthy.

I reached for a mug, hesitated, and grabbed a second one. I plopped a tea bag in each and filled it with hot water.

"There," I said, plonking one of the mugs in front of Felicity.

She gave me a strange look. "What's that?"

"Tea."

"I can see that," she responded dryly.

"Then I don't know what your confusion is about," I countered, grabbing my mug to retreat to my room. There was a limit to how much I cared about making her feel better and a cup of tea was about as much as I could manage.

I was halfway out when I heard a small voice behind me.

"Thank you."

Not sure what to respond, I just kept going, leaving Felicity to her thoughts. I glanced back but she just looked still, like a porcelain doll frozen in time. So strange.

After my shower, I checked the kitchen again but Felicity was gone. I could hear some faint music coming from behind her door when I returned to my room, which I took as a good sign. Hopefully, she'd be her usual, snarky self in the morning and I wouldn't have to clean the unicorn stable by myself.

If we were better friends, I might've checked in with her again but I didn't feel confident enough to step into her lair. I might never come out.

Come morning, the nice weather had turned and a miserable drizzle soaked everyone and everything around me. Luckily, there were raincoats available for the staff but I only got my hands on one after I arrived, drenched to my underwear.

Shivering, I waddled to the staff room where I spotted Felicity. Somehow, she'd stayed dry and looked her usual, condescending self. There was more spring in her step and her hair was tied up in a high ponytail that highlighted her laser-focused look.

Felicity was back.

"Out of the way, airhead," she sneered as she waltzed past me so she could reach Nissan first.

Followed closely by Aaron, I hurried towards our mentor so I wouldn't miss anything or look bad. I didn't know why she'd been so down yesterday or what brought her back, but I didn't care. My rival was back in shape which meant the competition to be number one was back on.

I only listened with half an ear to the other keepers, not able to remember everything going on in the sanctuary. We didn't even have to be in these meetings but if I wanted to get a permanent job here, it would be good if people knew who I was.

"Unicorns?" Gwen asked, grabbing my attention.

Nissan clicked his pen a couple of times. "No issues to report. We've finished preparing the quarantine bay and we need a new order of straw."

"Excellent. We're not sure when they're sending

the newcomer over but it'll be in the next couple of days." Gwen made herself some quick notes and turned her attention to the keeper next to us. "Lander? How are the phoenixes doing?"

A man with a low voice answered. "Nesting season is around the corner. We're hoping our breeding pair will give us some nice eggs."

Ooh. I wanted to see phoenix eggs. They were some of the most glorious birds out there, only rivalled by the thunderbirds. It would certainly be amazing to see one up close, feel the heat of their regenerative fire on my skin. Despite working at the Sanctuary, I hadn't had much time to visit the other enclosures and habitats. There was always something to do at the unicorns and when I wasn't shovelling poop, I was passed out in my bed. I had a free day coming up soon so hopefully, I could visit the rest of the zoo and get a good look at the other animals. But that was for later. Right now, the unicorns were probably desperate to go outside so we had to prepare their breakfast. With the meeting over, everyone returned to their respective habitats.

The signature snorting and clanging of hooves on a hard floor was audible way before I entered the stables. Nissan and Aaron did the perimeter check, making small repairs to the fencing, while Felicity and I fought over who got to prepare their breakfast. A nice difference from yesterday where she'd barely cared. When I applied to work here, I hadn't expected to become a personal caterer to the unicorns but it was fun to weigh out their purple carrots and watch them feed. By now, I was getting pretty good at keeping them all apart.

When Nissan was confident everything was secure, we let the unicorns out. The most infuriating part about Felicity's brash cockiness was that she lived up to it. She was efficient, methodical, and annoyingly, we worked well together. The competition drove me to perform better and I assumed it was the same for her.

The gate slid open and excited to be out in the sun again, Sunshine pranced out demonstratively. She really lived up to her name.

"They're so gorgeous," I mused as the silver blushes took to their breakfast like champions. The twins, Criss and Cross, ended up eating the same carrot and when neither wanted to let go, it snapped it in half.

Next to me, Felicity sighed dreamily. "Aren't they? They're so elegant and majestic. Even those cheeky boys. They have so much personality too."

"They do! You could tell me a story and I'd know

which unicorn did it." Our eyes met and my cheeks heated as I realised who I was talking to. What was I doing being friendly with my rival?

We quickly shuffled apart and observed the herd in silence. Closest to us, Candle daintily chomped on an apple. She was such a picky eater sometimes, if she was a human, she'd eat with silver cutlery and porcelain plates, only tasting the finest of foods. All the finesse was lost on The Sergeant. He devoured as much of the vegetables as he could, not afraid to chase the twins or Jun-Jun away. He eyed up Sunshine's stack but decided against it. Smart lad. Despite being the lead stallion of the herd, it was a bad idea to piss off Sunshine.

The herd finished their breakfast and retreated into the meadow, leaving us with more presents. After a week working here, the routine was becoming easy to predict. I could see how for some people, this could become boring but I knew there were so many more things we'd get to do once we were settled in a bit more.

Nissan just finished the logbook when his radio crackled and Gwen's voice came through the speaker. "Gwen to Nissan. I just got notified, the new unicorn is arriving today."

My eyes widened. Today? That was much sooner than planned.

"Nissan to Gwen. We'll give him a warm welcome," he responded, putting his walkie-talkie away. He turned to the three of us, the excitement on his face contagious. "Alright, sounds like our newcomer will be here a little earlier than predicted. Before they can join the herd, he'll have to be quarantined so the vet can make sure he's in good health. Let's work hard here so we can make the transfer as smooth as possible."

He didn't have to say that twice. Aaron, Felicity, and I shot into action and cleared up the stable in record time. We were about finished when Gwen called us to quarantine to help unload the newest unicorn.

I was beyond excited as the four of us made our way over to the loading dock, packed tightly in raincoats to protect us from the storm. A large trailer was already waiting and a handful of other keepers had shown up to assist. The miserable weather was soaking the ground and making it much harder to communicate.

"Right, let's get our new friend off the truck. He's been in there for about ten hours now, I'm sure he's dying to stretch his legs," Nissan shouted, waving to get the attention through the curtain of rain. "I need two of you to open the loading door. Felicity, Aaron."

The two other interns bolted towards the heavy doors and slowly pulled them open. The truck reversed towards the gap and halted right in front of the dock, water pouring off of the side.

The movement and the rough winds made the trailer wobble and the unicorn released a panicked whinny. I could hear his trampling hooves as he bumped into the sides, making it shake even more.

This would've been so much easier if it was nice weather.

"Give me a hand," Nissan called to me.

I rushed forward, eager to play my part. There was no way of knowing how this new unicorn would react so to be safe, we opened the designated area and closed off any other escape routes. Worst case scenario, the unicorn could bolt out of the trailer but then he'd run straight into his paddock.

Nissan beckoned at the driver. "Little more, little more. Perfect. Stop. Alright, ready to open the trailer?"

"Ready," I confirmed.

To ensure our safety, there were oversized padded pallets for us to hide behind, in case the unicorn decided to charge at one of us. Their kick was immensely powerful and their sharp horn could do some serious damage.

"Ready!" Nissan pulled the sliding lock and opened the doors of the trailer. From where I was standing, I didn't have the best vision of the animal inside but I could hear the familiar snorts and the kind of stumbling that you only got with big beasts.

Tense seconds passed without the emergence of our newest unicorn and Nissan and I exchanged a worried look, just as we heard another stumble. Hesitant hooves on the metal ramp, leg by leg, a white unicorn gingerly made his way down the trailer. One of the doors shrieked slightly and the silver blush jumped halfway into the paddock. With wide eyes, the newcomer slowly took in the environment, giving me my first good look at him.

The first thing I noticed was the short stump on his head.

Nissan's reaction mimicked my own. "Aww, you poor guy. You look so sad without your horn. Don't worry, you can grow it back safely here."

The driver had come to take a look as well and he seemed surprised. "I thought unicorns were supposed to have horns."

"They sawed it off at the reserve." My mentor grunted as he closed the trailer. "It's to discourage poaching. It's done in really high threat areas but it's only a bandaid. The real problem is the black market for unicorn horns. It's said to have magical properties but in all my fifteen years of working with silver blushes, I've never seen any evidence it's real." He stepped in to guide the unicorn towards the pen. "Lots of them get shot just for their horn so removing it makes him a less desirable target. Mind you, some people would still kill this beautiful beast for a small stump like that. Despicable."

I'd never heard Nissan speak this passionately about something and it was reassuring to know he felt the same about the unicorn preservation cause as I did. I'd definitely chosen the right place to intern.

I glanced at the unicorn's stump. It would eventually regrow into the majestic horn that everyone associated with unicorns, but right now, it was evidence of the ugly world he lived in.

"Easy, easy," Nissan tried, speaking in a low voice to keep the colt from startling even more. "Nice and easy, big boy."

We approached, pushing the soft pallets in front of us to back the unicorn into his enclosure. Reluctantly, he scraped his hooves along the floor as he retreated. Since I was closest to the door, I pushed it shut and slid the lock into place.

With the unicorn safely in his enclosure, I relaxed. That was a big task but we managed it.

"Let's have a look at this handsome fellow," Nissan said, checking the paperwork. "Hello, friend. Welcome to the Griffin Sanctuary."

"What's his name?" Aaron inquired as he and Felicity joined us by the fence.

"He doesn't have a name. He was brought in from the Dwensel Plains. They found him emaciated and alone. There was a recent poaching attempt so they believe he might've escaped. For his safety, they brought him here." Nissan flicked through the notes and hummed. "Alright, we'll get Jacob to check him out and see if he can give us a better estimate of age. They think he's between five and eight, so that's not much to go on."

"Is that the new unicorn?" a voice sounded from behind us.

I searched for the sound of the voice, matching it up with Starlise. She joined us by the fence, accompanied by another woman around her age and a disinterested Reya.

Nissan nodded. "Yes, that's our new colt. As you can see, he's not in great shape."

"Poor thing," the second woman said softly. "Has the vet been called?"

"Yes, he's on his way," the keeper responded. "It's been a while since we had a new addition to the unicorn herd."

"Right... Not since the twins," the woman noted.

She seemed up to date with the affairs of the Sanctuary so if I had to hazard a guess, that was probably Ella, the co-owner of the place and wife to Starlise. Those two started the sanctuary over twenty years ago and had grown it into the institute that it was now. Two formidable women and definite role models. I hadn't expected to meet both directors so soon so this was incredible. I had so many questions I wanted to ask them but that was not my place.

I turned my attention back to the emaciated colt, wishing we could do something about his shaking legs or miserable look. His soulful eyes were wide and filled with sadness. Maybe I was projecting that onto him, knowing his circumstances, but the ribs poking through his skin and his ruffled coat didn't lie. This was not a healthy, happy animal and surely, he was in pain.

Regardless, I could tell that once he was better, he'd be a beautiful unicorn. His coat was almost pure white, bar the grey patch on his forehead.

"He's a bit funny looking," Reya voiced from

behind her phone. "Look at his head, it's like someone put a sticker on him."

Starlise chuckled, not bothered by her niece's comment. "It does look a bit like that. Sticker would be a cute name for him. What do you think, Ella?"

The other woman spoke, confirming my guess about who she was. "I like Sticker. It suits him. Oh, there's the vet. Alright, let's give Jake some space so he can work his magic and get this handsome guy in tip-top shape."

If it had been up to me, I'd have kept Sticker company but I wasn't going to disobey an order from the director. That was a sure-fire way of getting me kicked out of the intern program.

With a last look at the sad unicorn, I made a silent promise that I'd be back to see him soon. With an endangered species like the silver blushes, every animal counted towards their survival. It would be incredibly tragic if Sticker died here and I was going to do everything in my power to make sure that wasn't going to happen.

EIGHT

With the new arrival, our daily tasks were a little different than the past week. Almost every task had doubled and the fact that there were four of us was coming in handy. We had our hands full keeping the paddock clean, repairing fences, preparing breakfast, and all sorts of grunt work that meant Nissan was available to take care of Sticker.

I wished I could be helping out with the new unicorn too but it made sense that he was doing such an important task himself.

At least we were allowed to go into the working area with the unicorns to feed them.

I held out a purple carrot to Sunshine, making sure to keep my palm flat. She snorted softly as her large lips picked up the treat.

"Good girl," I told her, resisting the urge to give her a stroke. Even though we were allowed to be in here with them, we were supposed to keep the contact to a minimum. Even during training, it wasn't like handling horses. Even with their approval, the unicorns were unruly, much less obedient, and the group dynamic added another layer of trickiness to everything.

But since these individuals would never return to the wild, it was a good thing if they got used to having keepers around, in case they needed to be handled or checked by the vet.

"It's a nice day. You must be loving the sun."

Sunshine nodded her head like she agreed but it was probably a coincidence. She brought her large head closer to me, sniffing in search of another carrot. She gently nudged my pocket, bringing her horn dangerously close to me.

I held my breath as I tossed the carrot to the side so she'd give me some space, only daring to breathe when she walked away.

That was a little too close for comfort.

I never expected I'd ever be in a situation like this. The fact that I was working with unicorns still baffled me. Unicorns! I was so freaking lucky.

From the right, Candle approached with a

curious look. She sniffed my shoulder and scraped her front leg through the sand.

"I'm all out of carrots." I held my empty hands up to show her. "Sorry, that's it for today."

She snorted in my direction and wandered off, joining her mother in search of more food. If we let them, they'd eat all day.

"Were you talking to the unicorns?" a voice to my left asked.

"So what if I was?" I returned, glaring at Felicity. Somehow, we'd drawn the short straw again and were stuck on shit-duty while Aaron got to help with Sticker.

Done with breakfast, we released the unicorns into the exhibit so the visitors could watch them graze and worked on cleaning out their stables. I was pushing a wheelbarrow full of straw out of the stable when I spotted a figure leaning against the side.

I didn't have anything nice to say to Reya so I wheeled past her with the intention of ignoring her.

"Glamorous," the teenager remarked, snickering from behind her phone.

I paused, reminding myself that she was the director's niece. I couldn't respond to her in the same way as Felicity. "What are you doing here?"

"None of your business. I can go wherever I want, my aunt owns the sanctuary."

"Strange to brag about that when you're disappointing her." Oops, that was much harsher than I intended.

Reya put her phone away, her eyes shooting daggers. "Excuse me?"

Well, I'd already spoken out of turn. A little bit more honesty wouldn't hurt. "It's obvious that Director Starlise loves this place and all the animals in it. We're all working hard to help these endangered creatures and here you are... playing games on your phone, looking down on us, and making snide remarks. Real cool."

As soon as the words left my mouth and I saw the figurative thunderclouds gathering above Reya's head, I knew I made a bad situation worse. I should've stayed silent. Humans were not my forte. That was why I worked with animals. Although that was no excuse for being bad at peopling. Especially in a place like this, where cooperation was at the core of everything.

"You're so rude."

"I'm just saying it like it is."

She scoffed. "I'm going to tell Aunt Starlise."

That was what I feared. Pretending I didn't care, I shrugged. "Okay. Whatever."

My disinterest only made the teenager more upset. "I mean it."

"Go right ahead," I bluffed, tightening my hands around the wheelbarrow's handles, pushing it ahead before I said more stupid things. I could feel my heart pounding between my ears from the encounter. I'd managed to play it cool but her threat hit home. If she got me fired, that would be the worst.

Felicity noticed my foul mood the moment I returned.

"Fell in the shit pile?" she asked as she looked me up and down.

"Ha, ha," I countered, trying to keep calm. I gathered a couple of breaths and pushed the conversation with Reya to the back of my mind. There was nothing else I could do so I couldn't let these worries affect my performance. Making mistakes would only make it easier for the Sanctuary to cut my internship short.

I straightened my back and dusted off my hands. "Are we done here?"

Felicity checked around. "Yup."

"Great." I reached for my walkie-talkie. "Charlotte for Nissan."

The speaker crackled. "Go for Nissan."

"We're all done with the morning routine. Do you need help with Sticker?"

"Yeah, I could use some more hands over here."

"Okay, we'll be there in a flash," I responded, turning to tell Felicity but she was already on her way, having left without me.

I hurried to catch the door and latched it on my way out. With the two of us doing the morning routine, we were a little ahead of schedule and had finished before the sanctuary opened to the public. In about half an hour or so, the first visitors would arrive to look at all our mythical animals and hopefully, make generous donations that would keep this place running.

Felicity and I walked through the sanctuary in silence, passing some of the ground crew who were doing a last check of the path for trash blown in or any potential fencing that needed repairs.

We arrived at the quarantine bay where we scanned our passes at the entrance and changed our shoes for sanitised boots. It was lively this morning, with all kinds of animal sounds greeting us as we ventured through the wide halls.

On my left, I got a glimpse of a mini-griffin pacing up and down his room, and on the right, two red kitsunes chasing after each other. I wasn't sure whether these nine-tailed foxes were new arrivals or maybe they were recovering after a vet visit, but it was good to hear their chittering. While sometimes it was an indicator of stress, it was usually a sign they weren't afraid and having a good time.

After we passed the smaller bays, we came to the larger pens. These were used to house some of the bigger animals, like the regular griffins, or some of the larger dragons, or in our case, a unicorn.

"Hey," I greeted Nissan and Aaron as I joined them by the metal enclosure that separated us from Sticker. "How's our newest arrival?"

"Not bad," Nissan answered, flicking through the chart. "The vet has just been to check on him and he seemed happy. We're still waiting on his blood results and we'd like to get him on the scale but he seems in an uncooperative mood."

"Anything we can do to help?" Felicity offered, glancing through the metal bars at the unicorn behind it. "He looks sad."

I agreed with her. When I looked into his large eyes, it felt like I could look into his soul. He must be scared being confined in this room when he was used to roaming free. Under different circumstances, if he wasn't so endangered, maybe there would be talk of nursing him back to health and releasing him but that would be like giving him a death sentence. There wasn't a meadow on the planet that was safe from poachers, even without his full horn. Some would have no problem killing him for the stump on his head, no matter how small.

"Hey, buddy," I said, greeting him softly. "I know it's scary but we're going to take good care of you, okay?"

Sticker snorted softly and scraped his hooves along the floor. His head bobbed up and down but beyond that, he wasn't moving much. Instead, he just remained in his corner, no doubt to protect his back.

Nissan put his chart on the clip of the stable door and hummed. "I want to start training him right away so we can hopefully weigh him in a couple of days when he trusts us more. Has any of you ever done any training with a unicorn or a wild animal before?"

"I did once, on a field trip," Felicity replied.

"We had an extra-curricular course. Evergreen University is very hands-on with this kind of thing," Aaron boasted.

All three sets of eyes turned to me and reluctantly, I shook my head. "I haven't... Or at least, not in an official capacity. I used to train my cat to shake her paw but now that I'm saying it, I realise it's not the same," I trailed off, wishing I'd kept out that last, pathetic part. That just made me sound even sadder.

Nissan smiled. "Actually, it's not that different. Sure, these wild animals aren't tame so there's no cuddling with them on the bed later, but the training, at least positive reinforcement-based training, is the same wherever. You ask an animal to do something, if they do it, they get a reward. Simple."

"I used to give my cat bits of fish," I added.

"There you go. For Sticker, we'll prepare chunks of purple carrot. Same as with the others. All unicorns love it but silver blushes especially." He looked around and grabbed a long stick with a red ball on top from the corner. "There we go. So we use this target to tell the animal what to do. Hold it out and when Sticker touches it with his nose, he gets a piece of carrot. Preferably, we'd do this in one of our paddocks but the quicker we can get him used to being here with us, the better. Here, I'll show you."

He grabbed the white bucket with the pieces of carrot and tossed them up, rattling the treats. From behind the fence, Sticker's ears twisted in our direction but he remained in his corner.

Nissan tossed a piece of carrot through the bars and unable to resist, the silver unicorn tentatively moved towards it. He gave the piece of carrot a good sniff before he lipped it off the floor, chewing it slowly. When Nissan rattled the bucket again, he seemed a lot more eager to get another piece of that.

Judging from his thin physique, he'd been food-deprived for a while before they found him. The lack of herd probably meant he couldn't graze safely, which caused his emaciation. That starvation prob-ably made these easily accessible treats all the sweeter.

It felt bad to exploit this animal's dire situation but this wasn't just to make life easier for us as a keeper. The easier it was to handle him, the less stress we'd cause if he needed to be checked out or needed some medication. Now that he was here, it was our duty of care to ensure he lived his best life. Just the lack of hunger or safety wasn't enough, we wanted to actively create an environment where he could thrive.

After feeding Sticker a couple of pieces of carrot, Nissan held the target out to the unicorn. Close enough to draw attention to it, not so close that it felt like a threatening gesture.

The white unicorn ignored the red ball and instead, kept his eyes firmly in the direction of the white bucket. He probably couldn't see the treats but he'd located them from the sound.

Nissan grabbed a piece of carrot and held it out, using the smell to guide Sticker to the target. Gently, the unicorn pressed his nose against the red ball and Nissan presented him with the carrot on the flat of his palm, but that was one step too far for our newest arrival.

His ears lowered and the unicorn took a couple of nervous steps back, scraping his hooves over the floor. A loud slam from somewhere else in the facility spooked him even more and he jumped back, getting as far away from us as possible. He bumped into the wall and with a loud whinny, he kicked his hind legs in the air and bolted to the other corner.

"It's okay, it's okay," Nissan tried, but his reassurance meant nothing to Sticker.

Growing more agitated with the minute, the silver blush kept racing from side to side, trampling all the straw, and bumping into the fence.

"Everyone out! Let's give him some space," Nissan ordered, gesturing for us to leave.

My heart broke for the distressed unicorn and I wished I could go up to him and give him a hug to let him know everything would be okay, but that would only freak him out more.

I followed Aaron and Felicity out, wishing we didn't have to put Sticker through this. Sometimes it was hard to remember they were wild when the herd was so accepting of the keepers coming in to feed them, but Sticker probably hadn't had many interactions with humans before. Poor thing.

"Well, that was dumb," Aaron complained grumpily. "He totally should've been more careful."

I eyed him up. "I think Nissan knows what he's doing."

"Then he should've known not to try and hand-feed a wild unicorn."

"Maybe he was testing to see how Sticker would react," I defended our mentor. Nissan's hands-on approach combined with his explanations made him an excellent teacher in my book. I was learning lots of new things every day and being thrown in the deep end meant I had to use all my wits to rise to the challenge.

"Whatever," Aaron huffed.

I glanced at Felicity, wondering if she was going to weigh in on our conversation but she just crossed her arms.

"I'm going to the cafeteria, I want coffee," she announced, turning on her heels and walking away without acknowledging either of us.

Aaron and I looked at each other and he shrugged. "I could do with coffee."

I glanced at the closed door of Sticker's enclosure and nodded. "If Nissan needs us, he'll page us."

We followed the blonde girl out of Quarantine, but that didn't stop me from worrying about Sticker. I really hoped we would be able to make him feel more settled soon. If the books were to be believed, too much stress for a unicorn could be detrimental and I wasn't sure what would happen if he collapsed in our care. That was easily the worst-case scenario and something I didn't want to find out any time soon.

A shiver ran down my spine, knowing that one day, I'd have to say goodbye to an animal and I pushed it to the back of my mind. That was the last thing I wanted to think about.

NINE

The next couple of days, caring for Sticker slotted into our routine. Slowly, the unicorn was gaining weight and starting to look healthier. His coat was getting that signature shine that made them look so elegant and he was a lot less skittish when it came to us. It was truly remarkable how quickly he was adapting but they were known for their intelligence. There was a good chance he was aware that we were helping him.

I hoped he knew.

His presence did mean more work for us, and that Nissan could only supervise at either the quarantine or the regular enclosure, but it gave Aaron, Felicity, and me a great chance of showing our qualities. We probably got more autonomy than usual interns and as much as I hated to admit it, we were all thriving. Aaron strutted through the sanctuary like he was already a permanent member and Felicity was even more swift to show off her knowledge. Considering they both came from all-star universities, that was to be expected. They did seem surprised that I was keeping up with them and if I was honest, I was a little surprised too.

But as I swiped my ID badge through the scanner at the Quarantine bay and changed my boots to bring Sticker his breakfast, there was no denying that I was killing it.

I made my way down the hall, checking out all the other rooms. The mini-griffin had moved on to the griffin house where it was joining the herd and was replaced by a rather aggressive chupacabra. With dark fur and a single menacing fang, it glared holes in my head as I passed it. I was sure it was more charming than it was presenting himself right now but I didn't care for it.

The two red kitsunes were still there, playing and wagging their many tails. From the morning meeting, I'd learned they were being transferred to a special kitsune reserve as a new breeding pair in the hope to establish a new population. It was funny to think that these adorable, mated-for-life, ginger foxes with their long noses and nine tails could potentially save their species from going extinct but I really hoped they would.

I arrived at the unicorn pen and pushed the heavy sliding door open. Sticker snorted in response and scraped his hooves along the floor.

"Hello, Sticks." I rattled the bucket with carrots to get his appetite going. "How are you this fine morning, buddy? Feeling rested?"

The unicorn snorted softly, ignoring whatever I was saying in favour of the carrots in my possession.

"You're hungry? That's good. Hungry means you feel safe enough to eat, hmmm?" I tossed a chunk of carrot on the floor. The stump of his horn scraped along the fence as he bowed his head to eat it. His bare head looked so wrong, I wished I could magically grow his horn back for him. But that was not how things worked.

Munching on his carrot, Sticker looked up at me, his eyes shining with hope. I held out the target and he bumped his snout against it, softly exhaling on the red ball.

"Well done!" I tossed him another chunk, not making the mistake of trying to hand feed him. It would take a lot longer to get him to trust us enough for that.

I was almost finished feeding Sticker breakfast when Nissan and the vet, Jacob, arrived to check on the unicorn.

"He's looking good, eh?" Jacob noted, snapping on a set of medical gloves. He opened his case and pulled out a thermometer. "I'd like to take his temperature. How is he doing with having us in his vicinity?"

Nissan pulled a face. "Not great and considering you're going to stick that in his rectum, I don't think he'll be pleased."

As if he could hear us, Sticker snorted in our direction and trotted away to the corner. I wasn't surprised that he didn't enjoy having us near him. Even though we hadn't given him any reason to mistrust us, this small pen had to feel claustrophobic. The sooner he could be moved to the unicorn house, the better.

Jacob sensibly put his thermometer away. "We should get the test results back today so if he's in good health and not showing any signs of illness, it might be best to move him out."

"That's exciting," I noted.

"I'll notify you all when the results come in," Jacob said, grabbing a notepad from his white coat and scribbling down something. "Alright, I've got other animals to check in but let's hope we can relocate him soon. See you later. Nissan. Charlotte."

Nissan checked his watch and nodded. "Okay, we should go and prepare the enclosure for Sticker at the unicorn house. We have to introduce him gradually to the herd so we'll prepare a separate pen for him."

I refrained from jumping up and down. "So exciting. I hope he'll fit in with the group. He won't be rejected, right?"

Nissan thought for a moment as we made our way out of the pen. "Our herd has a good track record of accepting new members. Sunshine is a great lead mare and she's very welcoming. I'm worried about Criss and Cross. They're about the same age as Sticker and they might not be happy with another male in the herd. It's The Sergeant's job to put the young colts in their place but he's not the youngest anymore."

"Unicorn dynamics are like politics," I noted, stepping aside so he could slide the door shut.

"In a way. We can worry about it later, first, we have to make sure Sticker is healthy enough to leave Quarantine." Nissan waved me along. "Let's give him some space."

We made our way to the unicorn stables where

Felicity and Aaron were just about done with clearing out the stables.

"How are our silver blushes?" Nissan asked cheerily.

"All taken care of. We just finished cleaning out the pen but we still have to put fresh bedding in," Aaron answered, leaning on his shovel.

Nissan ran a hand through his short curls and hummed. "Alright, you two finish the stables. I'm going to check on the new area. Charlotte, you're with me."

I happily skipped along. It was always a good day when I wasn't on shit-duty and I was excited to see the extension they were adding to the unicorn exhibit. If Sticker was accepted in the herd, they needed a little bit more space so they were extending the meadow. Small renovations but it would take weeks of work from the builders to realise it. I couldn't wait to see what they came up with.

I followed Nissan into the enclosure, excited to be out with the unicorns in their habitat. I was so lucky that they accepted me. Although that didn't mean I could let my guard down. In the end, they would always put their herd first and if they perceived me as a threat, they would deal with me like one. I didn't want to think about how it would feel to be impaled by multiple horns and trampled by their hooves.

Luckily for us, the herd was grazing on the other side of the enclosure so we could get a good look at the extension without having to worry about them barging in. The area was temporarily cordoned off as the builders put up more fencing. They were also planting a handful of trees to provide shade and I spotted a mineral block that needed to be put up too.

"I think that looks really good," I said, looking at Nissan.

"Same. Our builders are great at their job. This extra space will ensure that the unicorns can spread out a bit more as they graze. Hopefully, that'll make it easier for Sticker to be accepted in the herd."

His radio crackled and a male voice came through. "Jacob for Nissan."

He pulled his walkie-talkie off his belt and brought it to his mouth. "This is Nissan."

"I just received Sticker's test result. They all came back clean so I'm happy to release him from quarantine," the voice answered.

"Copy that, we'll make preparations to transport him," he responded, putting his radio back on his belt and turning to me. "Heard that?"

I nodded, trying to contain my excitement. "So we can introduce Sticker to the herd now?"

"Gradually, but yes." Nissan grabbed his walkie-talkie again and pressed the button to change the channel. "Nissan for transport."

A couple of seconds passed before a woman's voice answered. "This is Cathy, what can I do for you?"

"I'd like to arrange transport from the quarantine bay to the unicorn house for a silver blush unicorn. Medium-sized trailer should do."

The speaker crackled. "When do you need it?"

"We're ready for him so as soon as you can."

"Alright... How's tomorrow evening? I think Dwayne can squeeze you in." the woman proposed.

"That works for us. Thanks, Cathy." He put his radio away and grinned at me, his face shining with child-like glee. "Looks like we have a unicorn to transport."

TEN

I counted down the hours until Sticker's moving date. After spending a good while in the Quarantine bay with little space and even less outside meadow to roam around in, he was finally being transported to the unicorn house. That meant big preparations were in order.

We waited tensely for the notification that the trailer had arrived at the quarantine. It took all our manpower to guide Sticker in and lock him up, ready for a trip to the other side of the sanctuary.

Since this was a rather precarious operation, we were doing it after opening hours.

Luckily, it was only a short drive for Sticker and we were ready to receive him at the stable. Nissan was just as giddy and excited as all three of us. We'd prepared a separate pen for him so we could safely introduce him to the rest of the herd and hopefully, they'd react well to him.

The sound of the trailer put us all in motion and just like we'd practised, we took to our tasks. Aaron was in control of the gates while Felicity was opening the pen. Nissan would make sure the trailer was positioned right and I'd help him guide out the unicorn. We all had to work together and coordinate or this would be a disaster.

"Little closer, little closer!" Nissan waved, guiding the driver in as he backed the trailer towards the stable. "Stop! That's perfect. Okay, Aaron, open the gates!"

Aaron strained as he slid the large doors open just enough that the trailer opening fit in. They were made in a way that they helped form a barrier for the animal so they couldn't escape to the outside.

On the other side of the stable, Felicity opened the gates to the pen. It was next to the one where the herd slept in so that they could communicate during the night and get used to each other's presence. A great place for Sticker.

"Alright, Charlotte, are you ready?" Nissan questioned from the other side of the trailer.

I nodded, reaching for the metal latch on my side. "Ready."

"Okay, slowly, please."

In unison, we pulled the latches back and lowered the ramp so Sticker could come out. I worried he'd be reluctant like last time but the unicorn strutted out without any hesitance. Slowly but confidently, he walked down the ramp and paused just outside of the trailer. He looked around, taking in his new surroundings.

"It's okay," Nissan said, stepping away from the trailer and grabbed the target stick with the red ball. "This way, big boy."

Sticker gave him a long look and set in motion, moseying over to his new pen. His muscles moved visibly under his silver coat and his ribs were barely visible anymore. A wave of pride washed over me knowing he was so much healthier than when he arrived here. He looked so much better and he was also a lot less skittish and nervous.

Nissan held out the target stick with the red ball. "Over here. That's it. Over here."

All our training paid off as Sticker walked in her direction, gently touching the red ball with his nose. He tossed a chunk of carrot in with him as Felicity locked the gates, securing him in his pen.

We all released a sigh of relief and Nissan congratulated us. "Well done, well done. Alright, let's call it for today and get out of here. I'm sure Sticker would like to get used to his new home in peace and quiet. Oh, and don't forget, you have your first evaluation tomorrow but I'm sure you'll all pass."

I gulped. I hadn't realised that would be so soon. Hopefully, they'd be pleased with my performance. Nervously, I raised my hand. "What happens if we don't pass?"

"It'll go on your track record and if you don't pass the next one, you're out."

I gulped again. "Out?" Well, that wasn't good. I'd have to make sure my bosses were happy with me. If I wasn't already working my ass off, I'd change gears, but there wasn't much else I had left to show off. I knew how to work with unicorns, I was good at my job. My people skills needed some fine-tuning but it wasn't like I was an unsociable ogre. I just wished I had more time to prepare.

Back at the dorm, a nervous energy hung between all the interns. It looked like everyone was dreading the upcoming evaluation and that made me feel a little less alone. It would've been nice if Tina was here so I could talk to her but her internship was keeping her just as busy.

I'd just have to get through the nerves by myself.

I glanced across the stone kitchen island where Felicity was preparing her microwave dinner on the counter. She struggled with the cardboard sleeve and stabbed her fork through the film on top with murderous intent.

Perhaps I wasn't the only one stressed.

"What are you having?" I inquired while sipping from my tea.

"Pasta," Felicity responded curtly as she whacked the plastic tray in the microwave.

Somehow, seeing her on edge made me feel better. Especially if I could get a little bit of teasing in. "Nervous for tomorrow?"

"No."

"Really? So that's always how you kill your dinner?"

The other girl glared at me, the murderous intent aimed in my direction. "I'm not nervous."

"If you say so."

She twirled her fork dramatically. "You're infuriating, did you know that?"

"Thank you." I finished my tea and got up from my seat to give it a wash. Except that the sink was packed full of dirty bowls, plates, and knives sticking up. "Ugh. Who keeps leaving dirty dishes in the sink?"

"I heard it's Peter," Felicity answered from by the microwave.

I paused, struggling to wash my mug. "Who's Peter?"

"Peter. Lives at the end of the hall. Always makes bad jokes? Smells like sausage? I think he's a phoenix intern?"

"No idea." I pushed some of his plates to the side and the water splattered up at me, soaking the lower half of my shirt. "Ah, come on!"

Felicity chuckled at my misery. "You got we-et."

"Ha, ha, so funny," I mocked, sticking out my tongue.

"Careful with that," Felicity threatened.

"What? With my tongue? Why? What are you going to do to me?" As soon as I said it, I realised how it sounded and I quickly averted my gaze. The light-heartedness ebbed away and a slightly uncomfortable silence settled between the two of us, only filled by the soft rumbling of the rotating microwave.

I stared at my hands. "I'm nervous."

The microwave beeped and Felicity pulled the steaming pasta out, not bothering to put it out on a plate. She carried it over to the kitchen island and dug into her dinner, not looking at me. "I'm nervous too."

"But it's not like we'll fail our evaluation, right? Nissan seems pretty happy with us," I argued, voicing my concerns.

Felicity chewed thoughtfully. "I bet Aaron isn't nervous."

"Yeah, he's too cocky for that. He probably thinks he's got us both beat. I hope I don't have to work with him after we finish our internships."

The other girl paused mid-bite. "I mean... not likely since there's only one permanent spot available at the unicorns."

I choked on my spittle. "What? Only one? How do you know that?"

"There's always only one spot. Did you not know that?"

"No! What, so you're saying only one of us will get a job? Regardless of how good we are?" I coughed, trying to dispel the air. "Well, that... sucks! Jeez, what am I doing here? I need to prepare."

Worried and muttering to myself, I made my way back to my room. If Felicity was right and there was truly only one spot available, out-performing the others was more important than ever. But how was I going to prove that I was better than the other two?

No matter how much I disliked them, there was no denying their competence.

I worried and pondered and prepared as best as I could the entire evening. I slept terribly, not managing to shake the nerves when I woke up the next morning. Almost aimlessly, I completed my routine, not managing to fully enjoy the beauty and mystique of the unicorns.

After we were done with our chores, they called us into the primary staff building where all three of us would be evaluated separately.

I paced back and forth through the waiting room, focusing on the geometric shapes on the blue carpet. I knew I'd been doing well during my internship but it was still scary to go into an evaluation. What if they didn't think I'd been pulling my weight? What if they'd only been paying attention to Aaron and Felicity? What if Reya actually told her aunt that I'd been a little pissy with her?

I bit my fingernails, trying to contain my jitters. Why did I have to go last?

Finally, the door swung open and Nissan's head appeared. "Come in, Charlotte."

At least there was one friendly face here. Technically, they were all friendly faces and people I worked with daily, but still...

I ventured into the room and took place in the only chair facing a long table with Director Ella, Gwen, and Nissan.

"Good afternoon," I said politely, hoping to start this off on the right note.

Director Ella flicked through some sheets and pushed her glasses up her head. "Charlotte from Ashway University. That's not a school we often work with. You're one of our only interns from there."

"Cool," I answered, my voice shaking from my nerves. Oh no, why did I say that? What a terrible way to answer.

She looked at me with stern eyes. "Hmm. So I've got Nissan's evaluations here from you from the past weeks. Before we go over those, I'd like to hear from you how you've been experiencing your internship."

"Oh. Ummm..." My head heated up as I tried to formulate an honest but eloquent answer. "I think I've been doing well. I'm familiar with the morning routine by now. I think the herd and Sticker are getting used to me feeding and training them. I'm trying my best so... Yeah... So... Good, I think."

Director Ella hummed and turned to Nissan on her right. "You've been personally supervising Charlotte. What do you think of her?"

"Well, Charlotte is a hard worker, that much is obvious. She's efficient and often goes the extra mile. I can tell she's doing a great job establishing a rapport with the silver blushes as well so I'm happy. I've got three stellar interns this year," Nissan answered.

A wave of affection rolled over me for my mentor. I looked up to him and it was great to hear that he was pleased with my performance.

"Gwen?"

The copper-haired woman checked some of her own notes. "I agree with Nissan. Charlotte is always on time for the meetings, she takes initiative, and she does seem to have that special touch with animals. I'm pleased."

"That's great to hear," Ella responded, scribbling down something on her sheet. "Right, looks like we're happy so far. Your next evaluation will be in about a month or so. Keep up the good work."

I waited nervously to hear more but when it became clear that the evaluation was done, I stood up, thanked all three for their time, and tried my best to walk out calmly. It wasn't until I was back in the waiting area that I felt a weight fall off my shoulders. I was so lucky that my hard work had been paying off, I could cry.

Instead, I made my way towards the wishing

fountain where Aaron and Felicity were waiting for me.

Surprised to find them still here, I joined them. "Hey."

"How did your evaluation go?" Felicity asked, not beating around the bush.

I drew a deep breath. "Good. They were pleased with my performance"

Felicity looked annoyed. "Looks like the bar isn't set very high then."

"Clearly, otherwise you wouldn't be here," I retorted quickly.

"I'm number one in my class," Felicity shot back.

I crossed my arms. "So am I."

She chuckled. "I meant number one in a school that actually matters."

Yikes. That was a low blow right into my insecurities. I wasn't sure if she knew I felt self-conscious about not coming from an elite school but that stung.

With as much confidence as I could muster, I puffed my chest up. "And yet, I'm here, aren't I?"

"Me-ow," Aaron interjected, hissing playfully and swiping his hand through the air like a claw. "It's so fun when you little ladies get catty. Quick, get in the fountain and wrestle. I love when two girls get hot and wet together."

Felicity's eyes shot daggers at him. "You're such a pig."

"Oink oink," he joked, not bothered at all.

"You're so disgusting," I added, shaking my head in disgust. "You do realise the two directors of the sanctuary are women and married, right? I wonder what they'd say if they heard you talk like that."

Aaron's boisterous smile immediately disappeared from his face and he gulped. "You know I'm just kidding around, right?"

"Find something funny to kid around then," I spat back, walking away so I didn't have to spend more time with him. If only my girlfriend was here, she always knew what to say.

ELEVEN

I arrived at the dorm, excited to call Tina so I could tell her the good news about the evaluation. I took a quick shower first and wrapped up in my towel, I rested on my bed while I dialled Tina's number.

The line rang once, twice, thrice, no answer. I stared at the phone as it went to voicemail and tried again, to no avail. Maybe she was busy.

Strange. I checked the time and her latest message to make sure I was calling at the right moment. We said we'd call tonight so why wasn't she picking up?

I'd just pressed the green button again when loud music blasted through my door. Great... What was that?

With my phone in hand, I threw on some

comfortable clothes and ventured out into the hall to investigate. The music and shouting seemed to come from the kitchen and when I arrived, the loud boisterous chatter and laughter immediately brought back memories of parties at the university. The usual chill place to hang had been transformed into a houseparty. There were bottles of beer and other liquors scattered all over the counter, stove, and island. If anyone wanted to cook or heat a meal, they had to wade through a sea of alcohol and people.

Interns all over the place were dancing to the music, shouting, and singing. The intimate atmosphere was certainly a bit too intimate for me. I barely knew a quarter of the people's names and knew even less than them well.

I spotted Aaron chatting up some girls by the couch so I made my way over to him. "What's all this?"

"It's a party!" he shouted back, swigging from a bottle of beer.

"I can see that but why?"

"We all passed our first evaluations. Isn't that cause for celebration? Come on, have a drink!" He downed his drink and aimed the bottle at an empty case, managing to throw it into one of the slots. The girls around him cheered and he grinned, clearly loving the attention.

"No, I'm busy!" I snapped back, retreating from the kitchen so I could talk to Tina.

I tried calling her a bunch more times, growing increasingly more annoyed. The constant music, laughter through the halls, and occasional crashes here and there painted a vivid picture of the party on the other side of the door. After trying to get in contact with Tina for about an hour, I tossed my phone on the bed and made my way to the kitchen. If I was going to be frustrated, I might as well have a drink in my hand.

Upon entry, I bumped into Felicity and she steadied herself against the doorway. "Watch it."

"Sorry." I glanced past her at the dancing bodies, wondering if I'd fit in even if I didn't know anyone.

"Are you joining the party?" Felicity questioned, raising a single eyebrow in the way she did best.

I nodded and gestured to the cocktail in her hand. "I suppose so. Where can I get one of those?"

She gave me a haughty look. "That's my own recipe made from various, expensive alcohols that I don't share with anyone. Get your own drink."

"I don't have any, I didn't realise there was a party," I admitted, scanning the room. There was a surprising amount of alcohol around but I didn't know the rules. Was I allowed to just grab a beer? Did I have to pay for it? It looked like everyone knew what they were doing and nobody had informed my socially awkward self.

Maybe I should've stayed in my room after all. I checked my phone to see if Tina had called me back yet, but nothing.

"I'll just grab a beer," I noted, stepping past Felicity to make my way to the kitchen island where Aaron was chugging a beer in one go.

Once he spotted me, he grinned. "Chaaaaarlotte! You're back! Couldn't stay away from me, huh?"

I pulled up my nose. "Gross."

He laughed. "Ah, lighten up. Here, have a beer!"

At least that solved how I was getting a drink. I stepped forward to accept the bottle when my phone vibrated in my pocket. I quickly whipped it out, desperate to talk to Tina. My hopes were crushed when I saw the notification at the top of the screen. Just a random spam email.

Disappointed, I put my phone back and accepted the beer from Aaron. "Cheers."

TWELVE

About an hour later, I found myself on one of the couches quietly sipping my drink. While I wasn't necessarily enjoying the party, the loud music filled the entire dorm so there was no use in trying to sleep or relax in my room.

I checked my phone while I sipped from my drink, wishing Tina was calling me back. I was getting worried but none of my calls were going through and all the messages were left on unread.

With a sigh, I blacked out the screen and observed the people around me, recognising a few faces here and there. As interns, most of us kept our assigned habitats so we didn't have much to do with each other.

Felicity flopped down next to me, her eyes glazed over slightly. "Whatcha doing?"

I checked my phone for any missed calls again and shrugged. "Nothing."

"Why do you keep looking at your phone?" Felicity asked, gesturing to the device in my hand.

"I'm waiting for a call from..." I hesitated, unsure if I wanted to share my relationship status with her. Then again, if she was going to discriminate against me for being in love with a woman, that would certainly not fly here. Not with Director Ella and Starlise.

"From?" Felicity prompted.

"My girlfriend," I answered, keeping a close eye on her face to gauge her reaction.

"Oh. I didn't realise you were in a relationship," she said, not sounding judgemental in the slightest.

"Yeah. Tina is doing an internship on the other side of the country so we're doing long-distance for a bit. We were supposed to call tonight but she's not picking up."

"And you're literally waiting by the phone instead of enjoying the party?" Felicity rolled her eyes. "Lame."

"So you're obviously single," I noted dryly. If she was in love, she'd understand that calling with my girlfriend was much more fun than being at a weird party with a bunch of strangers.

"Obviously. I had a boyfriend but he didn't want me to come out here because we'd be away from each other. So I dumped him. I'm not going to let anything hold me back or stand in the way of my career." She finished her drink and scanned the crowd. "Lots of good-looking people in here. Aaron is hot, don't you think?"

"He's not my type. And he's an ass."

The girl next to me chuckled. "He is. But he's stupid hot."

"He's stupid, alright," I scoffed, sipping from my drink. I couldn't believe a guy like Aaron was standing between me and my dream. He was qualified, there was no doubt about that, but he was such an ass.

"Cheer up, little lady," she joked, nudging my shoulder and waggling her eyebrows.

I groaned. "Nooo, don't. I hate, hate, how he calls us little ladies."

"You do?" Felicity screamed. "Me too. I hate it. It's so condescending."

"Little ladies," I mocked.

She snorted. "Liiiiitle ladies. I hate it. Hate it! What's that even supposed to mean?"

I gasped for air, choking on my laughter. I gave her a friendly swat. "Oh my god, stop it. You're killing me. Little ladies!"

She howled, hitting my shoulder. "He's such an asshole. Why are hot guys always assholes?"

My face wrinkled in disgust. "You really think he's hot?"

"Umm, yeah? Do you not have eyes?"

"I do have eyes. And taste."

"Ha. Ha." Felicity swigged from her drink. "You're so funny. Not."

"Really? You don't think I'm funny for a little lady?" I joked.

The other girl almost choked on her drink and swatted my shoulder again. "Are you trying to kill me?"

"Not as much as when we first met," I answered semi-honestly. While Felicity would never be someone I chose to hang out with, she wasn't the worst person I ever met. Sure, she was a bit stuck-up and a know-it-all, and she liked to be the best, but I was used to that by now. A bit of healthy rivalry never hurt anybody. And for the first time since I came here, I felt like we were bonding. Our dislike for Aaron was the one thing we agreed on, which gave him some use.

I glanced at Felicity, bemused by how tipsy she was. She was swaying back and forth, spilling her special cocktail all on the floor. The haze in her eyes made her look softer and more approachable. She felt warmer too. If things kept going like this, maybe we'd end up friends after all.

"What are you staring at?" the other girl asked, locking eyes with me.

"Nothing," I denied, quickly taking a sip.

Felicity released a little disbelieving hum but didn't press on. "So what are you into then?" She gestured to a group of interns. "Becky with the glasses? Ryan with the very, very tight pants. Or Teresa with the skimpy shirt."

"I told you I have a girlfriend so none of them."

Felicity laughed. "Booooring. Internships are the time to have fun. You know, Teresa swings both ways."

"I'm not going to cheat on my girlfriend," I countered, shaking my head in disbelief.

Felicity rolled her eyes. She downed the last of her drink and rose from the couch. "Let's go dance."

"I don't dance."

"Your loss." She shrugged as she walked away, mingling with the other interns so she could grind with two other guys.

Bemused, I shook my head. I could not get a feel for this girl. It was like there were two Felicities. A snobby and condescending version that hated my guts and another softer persona that felt like she could be my friend.

I remained by myself, watching the world move around me. Was Felicity right? Was I being lame for waiting by the phone instead of trying to make some friends?

If everything went well, I'd have to work with these people for years to come. Wouldn't it be better to start making some friends?

I glanced at my phone, the number of unaccepted calls taunting me. I didn't know what Tina was up to but clearly, whatever she was doing was more important than talking to me.

Annoyed, I pushed my phone in my pocket and got up from the couch, determined to mingle. A handful of people were playing some kind of game that involved empty cups and a ping pong ball. I observed for a little while, trying to work out the rules.

One of the guys noticed me. "You want to play?"

My cheeks heated up. "Ummm... I don't know the game."

"You've never played phoenix cup? It's super

easy. Come on, we need another player," he shouted, pulling me towards the table. "What's your name?"

"Charlotte."

"I'm Blake," he introduced himself. He gestured to a girl with dark curly hair. "This is Ramona."

I gave her a little wave. "Hey."

Not interested in pleasantries, Blake pulled me towards the table and gestured to the set up. "So phoenix cup is real easy. You just grab the ping pong ball and bounce it in one of these cups. Depending on which cup you hit, the other team has to drink the corresponding drink. The red cups are beer, the blue are wine, and then there's the champagne flute. If you can get the ball in that, the other side has to drink the fishbowl."

"What's a fishbowl?" I questioned.

He gestured to a tall glass with an undefinable colour. "A little of everything. The game continues until someone manages to get the ball in the champagne flute."

That sounded easy enough. I accepted the ping pong ball and took place on the narrow side of the table, joining him and another girl. The opposing team was comprised of two guys and a third girl, none of which I knew. Not that it mattered. They chanted encouragingly and I aimed the ball at one of the larger red cups.

With a confident throw, the ball soared to the end of the table and went straight into one of the blue ones.

My team cheered and howled while the other group wailed dramatically. They poured themselves a cup of red wine and passed it around, downing it incredibly fast. Once they finished their drink, they took our place at the table and aimed the ball too. It bounced once, twice, before landing in a red cup. They cheered while Blake and Ramona booed.

These people were really into their game.

Ramona uncapped a bottle of beer and took a large swig before handing it to Blake. He finished about half and passed the rest to me. I wasn't super crazy about sharing a drink with people I'd just met but then again, whatever.

I put the bottle to my lips and let the cool beer flow down my throat. I hated drinking beer this quickly but I wasn't going to let my team down.

Blake cheered when I handed him the empty bottle back and held out his hand for a high five. Encouraged by the excitement, I slapped his hand and focused my attention on the game. Whether this counted as mingling, I wasn't sure. But at least it was taking my mind off of Tina.

A couple of rounds later, my stomach was bloated from all the wine and beer. I wasn't sure exactly how much I'd drank but it was definitely a bit more than one drink to take the edge of.

Slightly swaying, I closed one eye to help my aim. I held the little ball between my thumb and index, flicking my wrist as I aimed it at the champagne flute.

The ping pong ball soared through the air and with a satisfying clink, it hit the rim of the flute, and bounced into another red cup.

"Ahhhh, so close!" I exclaimed, joining in with Ramona and Blake's disappointment. While there was nothing at stake, it was too easy to get invested in the game and now I wanted to win.

We played a bit more, drank more, until it was my turn again. I rotated my shoulder loose and pulled my arm back so I could get a good angle on my throw. I released the ball and almost in slow motion, I watched it soar straight in the champagne flute.

The group was silent for a moment before we broke out into victory cries.

"Phoenix!" Ramona cheered, pulling me into a hug.

"Phoenix!" Blake drummed his fist on his chest, continuing to chant. "Phoenix, Phoenix, Phoenix!"

The losing team didn't seem very happy that they had to drink the fishbowl but they were taking their defeat with dignity. Blake grabbed the glass with the weird concoction and before he handed it to the other three, he grabbed a lighter and set fire to the top of the drink. Blue flames danced on top of the surface as the members of the losing team each took turns drinking from the glass. The disgust on their faces made me really, really glad that I managed to secure the victory for us.

"Well-played," Ramona complimented me. "You're really good at this game. You only missed like twice."

"Thanks."

"What a sharpshooter!" Blake enthused, grabbing another bottle of beer and pushing it in my hands. "To victory!"

I put the bottle to my lips and that was one of the last things I could remember from that night.

THIRTEEN

The next morning, the dorm was really quiet and the smell of stale beer hung everywhere. The kitchen was a deserted battlefield of empty bottles, crushed packets of crisps, and cigarette buds. I wasn't sure who was supposed to clean this up but I wasn't going to tackle this on my own.

I grabbed some cereal and made my way back to my room so I could have breakfast in bed. I grabbed a bowl and spoon, only just realising I'd forgotten to bring milk. I got back out and came eye to eye with a barely-clothed Felicity sneaking out of... Aaron's room.

She spotted me and froze.

"Really?" I couldn't stop myself from commenting. "You slept with Aaron? Why?"

"None of your business," she sneered back, although some of its force was lost by how hungover she looked.

I didn't know why but I felt disappointed in her. She was always the first to tell Aaron to shut up when he said something rude and yet, she slept with him? Why were straight women always attracted to assholes?

Not knowing what else to say, I continued on to the kitchen to grab my milk. By the time I got back, Felicity was gone and her door was closed. Whatever, if she wanted to sleep with Aaron, that was her decision.

I sat on my bed and poured my milk on my cereal, desperate to get something substantial in my stomach that would soak up all the booze from yesterday.

Just before I took my first bite, my phone buzzed on my nightstand. Tina's name danced on the screen with a little green phone next to it.

Finally.

I picked up and pressed the phone to my ear. "Hey."

"Are you okay? I've been trying to call you all night," Tina shouted.

The loudness made me wince and I pulled the

phone back, putting it on speaker instead so I could hold it away from my ear.

"No, you haven't," I denied, checking the log, surprised to find multiple missed calls from my girlfriend. "Huh. You have. Weird."

"Why weren't you picking up?"

My head pounded, a reminder of last night. "There was a... An intern get together."

"So... you went to a party? I thought we said we were going to call," Tina accused me, her voice shrill.

Irritated, I pushed back. "Hang on. I tried calling you for hours. You didn't pick up, which is why I went in the first place."

The line crackled. "I got caught up at work. There was an emergency."

"Why didn't you text me?"

"There was no time, it was an emergency. I called you as soon as I could. I tried all evening, I wanted to hear your voice."

Thinking of Tina trying to call me all night made me feel bad for going to the party and having lots of fun. I should've stuck it out and waited after all.

"I'm sorry," I said, rubbing my head in the hope that the pending headache would go away.

"It's okay. I should've texted you. This long distance thing is hard."

I sprawled out on my bed and stared up at the ceiling. "So hard. I miss you."

"I miss you too. Did you pass your evaluation?"

"I did."

"Congratulations, Char!"

I winced from the loudness. "Thanks."

"You okay?"

"Yeah, just a little hungover," I admitted. "I played phoenix cup and although we won, I don't feel like a winner."

Tina's chuckle came through the speaker. "Ahh, yeah that game is deadly. Sounds like you had fun."

"I did." I said, thinking back to last night. I wasn't sure if I made friends with Blake and Romana but that was two more people that I knew. Maybe I could trade those two for Felicity and Aaron. Especially now that they were sleeping together. Barf.

"I'm glad." A knock came through the speaker and some muffled conversation that I couldn't hear. After a couple of seconds, Tina came back to the phone. "Char? I've got to go but we'll talk soon, okay. Tonight?"

"Okay, talk tonight. Love you."

"Love you too," she responded, ending the call.

I stared at my phone, not sure why I felt so empty. Maybe it was her tone, or just the brevity of our conversation, but I didn't feel the usual happy glow after we spoke. I didn't like that she made me feel bad about yesterday either, considering I tried to call her plenty of times.

With a sigh, I tossed my phone on my pillow and reached for my breakfast. The cereal had gone all soggy and I'd lost my appetite. I tossed it down the bin and went to work on an empty stomach. That was probably best, considering how run down I felt.

I DRAGGED my heavy body through the sanctuary, glad there were no visitors yet. I passed a small group of familiar faces from yesterday's party, although their names alluded me, and they gave me a nod of recognition. Looked like my socialising had paid off.

I arrived at the unicorn house, grunting as I slid the barn door open. My muscles were like pudding and everything felt twice as hard.

"Morning," Nissan chimed from behind his clip-board, chipper as always.

"Mmrrrning," I managed, trying my best to appear bright and upbeat. It was probably not the best work etiquette to show up hungover.

The door rattled again and Felicity arrived with

the same fake smile on her face. Looked like she was paying the price as well. She joined me to put on our work boots, grunting from the effort.

She looked at me. "Hey, about this morning—"

"About you coming from Aaron's room?"

Felicity sighed as she wrestled with her first boot. "Yeah, that. So I'd appreciate it if you kept that to yourself. I don't want our mentor to find out and treat me differently."

"Why would he do that?"

She gave me a look. "Men don't like the concept of women having one-night stands, except if they're the ones having the one-night stands."

"I'm sure Nissan isn't like that."

"Okay. Then I don't want our boss to know about my personal sex life."

I nodded. "Yeah, that's a fair point. Consider my lips zipped."

Felicity pulled her second boot on and continued on without so much as a thank you. She joined Nissan by the fence with her usual enthusiasm and shot me that challenging smile that infuriated me so much.

She really thought she was better than me, huh? Well, I was going to give her a run for her money. That top spot and the spot here at the Sanctuary were mine. If I was lucky, they wouldn't hire her and I'd get to work with the unicorns by myself.

Unfortunately that was quite a ways off and Nissan assigned Felicity and me to shit-duty. I wasn't very pleased after seeing her sneak out of Aaron's room so I'd much prefer to be somewhere she was not, but bringing that up to our mentor was bad form. Plus, Felicity did ask not to bring personal stuff up here at work. While I was upset with her, I didn't go back on my promises and I hoped one day, if the reverse was true, she'd grant me the same courtesy of keeping work and private life separate.

I ignored Felicity as I made my way to the stable. The sooner I got this done, the quicker I could get away from her.

Fueled by my irritation, I shovelled the unicorn poop and straw in the wheelbarrow. After doing this for weeks, my muscles were getting used to the intense labour and it wasn't nearly as hard anymore.

That didn't stop this from being one of my least favourite jobs. Life as a keeper was definitely less glamorous than I expected but it was all worth it. Getting to work closely with the unicorns was a dream come true. I really, really hoped I could continue to do well so the sanctuary would offer me a permanent position.

On the other side of the pen, Felicity dug her shovel in a heap of straw. "So... did you get in touch with your girlfriend?"

"I did, we called this morning." I kept working, not sure if I should elaborate more. I wanted to talk to someone about our conversation but was Felicity really the person I wanted to confide in?

Then again, I didn't have anyone else to talk to.

I paused for a moment, resting the pitchfork against the wall. "She tried to call me yesterday but I didn't feel my phone vibrate. I must've been too tipsy while playing phoenix cup. She was kind of mad that I'd missed our call."

"Really? But wasn't she the one that was late?" Felicity narrowed her eyes as she scooped up a bunch of poop. Her arms flexed as she dumped the load in the wheelbarrow. For someone that looked so dainty when she arrived, she'd put on a lot of muscle. I hated to admit it, but it looked good on her.

With a sigh, I kicked some straw to the side. "She said she had a work emergency."

"Hah. Work emergency."

I glared at the other woman, but she wasn't paying any attention to me. I leaned on my pitchfork, not liking the way she said it. "Why are you saying it in that tone?"

"I don't know." She wiped her hands on her over-all. "It's a lame excuse."

"I'm sure it's true."

"So naive. My dad used to cheat on my mum all the time. He'd always have some kind of work emergency which was code that he was busy doing his secretaries."

"Okay, Tina is not like that."

Felicity shrugged as she returned to logging our notes. "Alright, if you say so. I don't know her but she was late herself so it's real shit that she made you feel bad for not sitting by the phone all night like a good little housewife. You're allowed to have a life."

I chewed on my lip. What Felicity was saying made sense but that in itself was worrisome. What an upside down world.

Annoyed, I shoved my pitchfork in a bunch of straw and catapulted it towards the wheelbarrow. The clump hit the side and most of it went on the floor.

Even more irritated, I stomped over there and shovelled it in.

"You missed," Felicity noted dryly.

"I hadn't noticed," I responded, rolling my eyes as far into my skull as they went.

She thudded her shovel down. "Did you just roll your eyes at me?"

"Are you going to keep stating the obvious?"

She scoffed. "Hey, don't take your relationship trouble out on me."

"I'm not."

"Really? Cause you're acting like such a—"

"Bitch?" I finished her sentence, pausing my work so I could glare at her.

"That's not what I was going to say," Felicity denied.

I kicked some straw out of the way. "Then what were you going to say, huh?"

"Doesn't matter. The point is, you're being really unprofessional."

My hands balled into fists. She was calling me unprofessional? After she slept with Aaron and asked me to keep it a secret from our boss? Wow. Just. Wow.

To prevent myself from doing or saying something stupid, I turned around and pushed some more dirty straw into a heap. The metal tines of the pitchfork scraped over the stone floor as I picked up a pile of poop and aimed it at the wheelbarrow.

With too much force behind it, the clump hit the

metal rim and continued on, barreling towards the other girl.

"What the fuck!?" Felicity exclaimed as some of the unicorn poop splattered against her boots.

I winced. "Sorry."

"Did you just throw shit at me? What is your problem?"

"No, it was an accident."

With a scoff, she dug her shovel in one of the poop piles and hurled it my way. I threw my pitchfork down as I jumped out of dodge. Most of it missed but some of it splatted against my overalls.

My chest tightened in anger. "Are you serious?"

"You started it."

"I told you, mine was an accident!"

"Yeah, sure."

I stomped my foot. "It was."

"Please, you've been in a pissy mood all morning. Don't take whatever you're angry about out on me."

That was rich.

"I'm angry at you!" I hissed. It wasn't until the words left my mouth that they really registered.

Felicity threw her hands up in the air. "What? Why? What did I do?"

"You slept with Aaron." As soon as I said it, I realised how petty it sounded.

"So you're jealous?"

"I'm not jealous. I'm upset because..." I screamed in my hands, muffling the frustration so Nissan wouldn't be alerted. Or worse, Aaron.

"Because?" Felicity prompted.

"Because I thought we finally had something in common. Last night, at the party, we were bonding and getting along over our dislike of Aaron. It felt like maybe we finally understood each other. And then you slept with him. That's the opposite of disliking him!" I ranted, surprised to find Felicity calmed down.

She put her shovel down and ran a hand along her blonde ponytail. "Ah."

"Yeah. I know it's stupid but I don't make friends easily and I thought maybe, you know... You and I were becoming friends. I guess not," I muttered, feeling my cheeks heat up. It was embarrassing enough that I felt this way, but admitting it out loud made it sound even pettier.

Felicity sighed. "It might surprise you to know I don't make friends easily either."

"Yes, such a surprise," I noted sarcastically.

"Will you stop that?"

"Sorry."

The other girl stared at her hands for a moment,

her shoulders slumped. "If you must know, I didn't break up with my boyfriend cause he didn't approve of me coming here. He cheated on me and dumped me so he could be with his new girlfriend."

"Ouch."

"Yeah." She gathered a deep breath and sighed. "I slept with Aaron because I don't like him. I know that doesn't make sense but that's why I did it."

I took a step towards Felicity and shot her what I hoped was a reassuring smile. "It does make sense."

"Really." She shot me a disbelieving look.

I nodded. "Yeah."

Relief flitted through her eyes and her face softened again. "Thanks."

"I'm sorry your boyfriend was a jerk."

"Me too." She released a slight chuckle. "See, plenty of annoying people we can bond over."

I returned her smile. "Does that mean you want to be friends?"

"You make it sound like we're ten." She picked up her shovel and returned to cleaning out the stable. "But fine, we can be friends."

My smile grew into a massive grin as I continued filling the wheelbarrow. I felt bad that I threw poop her way but it looked like it at least cleaned the air between us.

"I wonder what the animal behaviourists would say about two keepers flinging faeces at each other," I mused out loud.

"And over a boy, nonetheless. They'd have a field day," Felicity chuckled as she cleared the last of the bedding from her side. "That's me all done."

"Me too." I put the pitchfork down and gestured to the overflowing wheelbarrow. "Since we're now friends, you'll empty it, won't you?"

With a scoff, Felicity turned on her heels and marched out of the stable. "We're not that good of friends."

FOURTEEN

Life at the Sanctuary continued in both an unexpectant and monotonous way. There was our daily routine that consisted of the same tasks and then there was the element of surprise that turned every day into an adventure.

Despite our differences, Aaron, Felicity, and I worked well together and under Nissan's supervision, we had the unicorn house running smoothly. The long hours left little time for a personal life but I managed to cultivate some friendships, although my calls with Tina suffered. The night of the first party wasn't the only time we missed each other and it wasn't the last. The more days passed, the less time we seemed to have for each other. Our schedules were mismatched and there weren't many days that we had lunch at the same time.

I chewed on a piece of toast, enjoying the sun. It was likely to be one of the last warm days of autumn so we had to take advantage of being able to have lunch outside while we could.

Over the weeks, my little group of people I knew had grown and when their schedules allowed it, Blake or Ramona often ate lunch with me. Today, surprisingly, both of them were on the same shift and had joined the same table as Felicity and me.

"Strawberries are one of Summer's favourite snacks," Blake said between bites of his sandwich, as always, talking about his dragons. "She also loves corn kernels. She makes them pop with her fiery breath, isn't that fun?"

He really loved those creatures.

Ramona chuckled as she bit into her stone fruit. "Very fun. Mmm, these are so good. I can't believe they're not imported."

I turned out the random conversation in favour of my phone. While I enjoyed the light casual chatter, this was one of the rare moments I was actually able to text Tina.

My phone vibrated and a message from Tina rolled in. <Good news! My supervisor said he's

pretty sure there will be a job for me here. Isn't that amazing?>

I typed a reply back. <That's amazing. I'm so proud of you. We should celebrate. Are we still on for our call this weekend?>

"Charlotte. Charlotte? Charlotte!" Felicity jabbed her elbow in my side to get my attention.

I looked up from my phone. "What?"

"Blake said there's a party this weekend and wants to know if you're free," she inquired, gesturing to the guy on the other side of the table.

"No, I'm face-timing with my girlfriend—" my phone buzzed as Tina's latest reply came in. I sighed and put the device away. "Actually, I am free, after all. Where are we going?"

"The Jungle. It's got the best music," Blake said, swinging his arm around Ramona's shoulders. "And we want to dance."

"Sounds good," I responded, trying to sound chipper. This was the fourth day in a row that Tina didn't have time to call and it was getting to me. We'd barely spoken, barely texted, and it felt like a whole world of new things was happening on her side of the country that I wasn't a part of.

"You look sour," Felicity noted, gesturing to my phone. "Girlfriend troubles again?"

"You and Tina having problems?" Ramona added, leaning in with much interest.

"Oops, girl talk." Blake grabbed his tray and climbed out of the picnic bench. "That's my cue to leave. Byeee."

With his departure, the two other girls only seemed more intent on finding out what was going on in my love life.

"Well?" Ramona prompted.

I sighed and pressed my head in my hands. "It's nothing, Tina and I are just struggling to find time to call."

Next to me, Felicity expelled air. "Pssh. To make a long distance relationship work, you don't find time. You make time."

"Okay, we're struggling to make time then. What's the difference?" I snapped back. Despite Felicity and I becoming friends, not much had changed in our dynamic. Our competition was as fierce as in the beginning and we engaged in a no-holds-barred type of honesty that bordered on tactless.

The blonde girl shrugged, not bothered by my sharp tone. "Priority. Maybe your relationship is no longer that important to either of you."

"Excuse me, Tina is the love of my life," I bit back. "Our relationship is really important."

"If you say so."

"I mean it. She's just really busy with her internship and I respect her space."

Felicity picked out the tomatoes in her salad and pushed them to the side. "Okay."

"I'm going to marry this woman."

"Okay," she replied with a bored tone. "I believe you."

"You don't sound like you do," I countered, jabbing my straw into my juice box.

"Why does it matter if I believe you anyway?"

Before I could answer, Ramona snickered from across the table. "You two bicker like an old married couple."

I stared at her, letting her words sink in. "What?"

"Yeah. You remind me of my grandparents." She finished her lunch and grabbed her tray as she got up. "Adorable. Anyway, I'll see you tonight! Party! You're coming, right?"

"Sure, sure," I answered, waving her out. "I could use a drink."

"Great." Ramona flashed us a smile. "Byeee."

Felicity picked at her salad until the other girl

was out of earshot. "Do you think she and Blake are hooking up?"

I paused to think about it. "Huh. I hadn't considered that but they sure are close."

"I think they are. They have that vibe." She pulled a face as she ate one of her vegetable cubes and shuddered. "Yuck. I hate milk root."

"Then why did you get a milk root salad?"

"I like everything else that comes with it," she said, pushing the white cubes to the side. "I'm sorry your relationship with Tina isn't going well. Even airheads like you deserve love."

I ignored her insult, which had almost become endearing, and slurped the last of my juice. "It just seems that she never has time lately."

"I bet she has time right now."

With a glare, I crumpled my juicebox. "I told her I had my break so if she does, she'd already have called."

"Yeah. Sure."

"You don't know her," I defended my girlfriend. I didn't like the low opinion Felicity had cultivated about her.

Felicity finally stopped pretending she was eating her salad and stole a sandwich from my plate. "Does she get jealous easily?"

I shrugged. "Not really. Why?"

She held out her hand. "Give me your phone."

"No." I clamped the device protectively against my chest. I wasn't going to give Felicity access to it.

"Just give it to me," she said, her tone bored. She reached over me and with her long arms snatched the phone out of my hands. Without waiting, Felicity swung her arm around me and dropped her head on my shoulder. With her free hand, she held out my phone and snapped a quick selfie before I really realised what happened.

"What are you doing?" I questioned, trying to ignore the sweet floral scent coming from the other girl. She smelled nice, especially in combination with some of the blooming trees around.

"Getting you on the phone with your girlfriend." She tapped the screen on my phone and smiled as she handed me the device back. "Voila."

Eagerly, I took it back and looked at the screen. She'd opened my social media and dropped the picture on my wall with a simple caption. Chilling with Felicity.

"What's that for?" I questioned, staring at the picture she just snapped. We were a little off-centre but I could tell her arm was wrapped tightly around me. Her dazzling smile made it hard to look at anything else and nobody would've been able to guess that we didn't get along.

Before Felicity could answer, my phone buzzed and Tina's name appeared at the top.

"Told you," the girl next to me sang.

I shushed her so I could pick up the phone. "Hello."

Tina ignored my greeting. "That's Felicity?"

"Yes. Why? Is that a problem?"

"You didn't tell me she was this hot!?"

I glanced at the woman next to me. Sure, she was pretty. Her blonde hair was nice and shiny, and she had those big eyes that made her look a bit like a peryton doe, but why did that matter?

"I thought you said you didn't have time to call until after the weekend," I pointed out.

The line was silent for a moment. "I don't. I cut my lunch short so I could talk to you."

I frowned. "So you could call to point out my friend is hot but not to chat?"

Next to me, Felicity waggled her eyebrows smugly and I pressed my finger against my lips, hoping that would shut her up. While I didn't like the conversation I was having with my girlfriend, at least I was having one.

Tina's voice came through the speaker. "I thought you said you didn't like Felicity."

"I don't. She's barely a friend."

Felicity fake-gasped and dramatically grabbed her chest.

With a glare, I got up from the picnic bench so I could talk to my girlfriend in private. There was an empty bench near the bin without any people around. I sat down at the end, my phone pressed tightly against my ear. "You don't have to worry about a thing," I reassured Tina.

"Really." The disbelief dripped off her voice. "You two look very cosy to me."

"It was just a fun picture. It doesn't mean anything."

"Is she into girls?" Tina asked sharply.

"Why does that matter? She knows I'm in a relationship," I articulated, not liking where this conversation was going.

Tina scoffed. "That doesn't stop a lot of people."

I frowned. What's that supposed to mean?

"I'm just saying."

A real nauseating feeling churned through my stomach. I barely managed to splutter out the question but I had to ask. If I didn't, I'd be up all night wondering about this. "Are... Are you cheating on me?"

"What? No! Why would you ask such a horrible thing?"

"You just said— But you— And Felicity said—"

"Oh my god, will you just shut up about Felicity. The entire month it's been Felicity this, Felicity that. I've had it up to here hearing about bloody Felicity!" Tina hollered through the phone.

I ground my teeth together, not appreciating her tone or what she was saying. I hadn't talked that much about Felicity and that was beside the point. Why was she upset with me when she was being unreasonable? Why were we wasting what little call time we had on a fight about nothing?

Before I could formulate an answer, Felicity appeared next to me. She emptied her tray in the bin and wordlessly tapped her watch.

I checked the time, realising our lunch break was almost over. I interrupted whatever Tina was saying, knowing I had to get a move on or I'd be late. "Can this wait? I have to go."

"What? No, we're in the middle of something."

"I'm sorry but I have to go. We have another evaluation coming up soon so I have to be on the ball."

"Charlotte. We're not done. Don't you dare hang up on me."

"I'm sorry."

"Charlotte. Charlotte!"

I ended the call. I hated that I just hung up on her but this call was getting out of hand and I couldn't afford to be late. I'd worked too hard to show Nissan and my bosses that I was responsible and great at my job. I wasn't going to throw that all down the drain by letting personal drama interfere with my work. No matter how awful it made me feel.

FIFTEEN

Felicity kept eyeing me up on the way back to the unicorn house. A couple of times, it looked like she wanted to say something but she didn't. Maybe I should blame her for posting that picture of us but what would that accomplish? It was just an innocent picture between two colleagues. It didn't mean anything so Tina was just being unreasonable.

We arrived at the stable where Nissan was waiting for us.

I glanced around, surprised to find it was just the three of us. As much as I disliked Aaron, I couldn't fault his work ethic and he was never late.

"Where's Aaron?" I inquired.

Nissan looked up from his chart. "Oh, they

needed some extra hands with the meadland ponies so I loaned him out."

"Oh." I recalled when he said those animals were difficult for interns and wondered if any of us had been up for consideration. Or had Aaron's fancy education given him a leg up?

I glanced at Felicity, hoping to read her face but she didn't seem bothered. Then again, she was good at hiding her true feelings. For all I knew, she could be boiling on the inside.

Clueless, our mentor gestured to the exhibit. "We're introducing Sticker to Jun-Jun today. Let's get one of the pens set up so they can meet through the fence."

"Yes, boss," I answered, saluting somewhat sarcastically. He shot me a weird look but didn't question it. Luckily.

Felicity and I made our way to the stables to set up the area.

"Guess it's just us." She gave me a little elbow jab as she continued in a singy voice. "Hope your girlfriend won't get jealoussss."

I swatted her shoulder. "Stop it."

She stuck out her tongue and sent sarcastic air kisses my way.

"I said stop it. I'm serious. It's not funny. I think we're breaking up."

That stopped her in her tracks. A guilty look flitted across her face. "Oh. I'm sorry, I didn't realise. I thought it was just one of those rough patches where you were just missing each other."

"We are. I think. I don't know." I opened the gate so we could go into the working area. "Recently, we've just been fighting a lot."

Felicity kicked a bit of straw to the side. "I'm sorry. If I knew, I wouldn't have posted that picture of us."

I secured the fence. "It's not your fault. Things haven't been good for a while and Tina is being unreasonable. She knows I would never cheat and I told her you're not into women so I don't get what she's getting so upset about."

The other girl tilted her head. "What makes you think I'm not into women?"

"Well, umm... You hooked up with Aaron so I just assumed..."

She clicked her tongue rapidly. "You shouldn't assume. People can like more than just guys or girls."

I did a double-take of the girl next to me, seeing her in a new light. "Huh."

"You could try to sound less surprised," Felicity grumbled.

"Sorry. I just didn't get that vibe from you."

"That's because humans don't communicate through electromagnetic pulse. We're not krakens."

"You know what I mean."

"Yes, I do. You're talking about outdated, harmful stereotypes. And here I thought you were more advanced than Aaron."

I scoffed and jabbed my elbow in her side. "You take that back. I'm nothing like that caveman."

"Ouch. You hit me." She swatted my shoulder in return.

"Hey! Why did you do that?" I countered, shoving her while I pretended to be hurt. The slight sting was already gone but that wasn't the point. This was about principals.

Before she could retaliate, Nissan entered the enclosure. He brought a bucket with purple carrots along and put it down next to us. "I think we should introduce Sticker to Jun-Jun first. I don't foresee any aggression between the two of them."

I nodded. "Which one do you want us to bring here?"

"You two should do Jun-Jun. I'll release Sticker once you've brought the mare here."

Felicity and I nodded, each grabbing some carrots from the bucket. It wasn't entirely ideal to go out into the exhibit with the herd but by now, they were pretty used to us as keepers. It shouldn't be a problem and their behaviour was more predictable than Sticker's.

We ventured out into the meadow, the argument ceased. Out here in the exhibit, both animals and keepers were on display to the public. It would reflect badly on the Sanctuary if we were bickering so we had to keep any personal conflict backstage.

"It's a beautiful day," Felicity mused, staring up at the clear sky. "I'm sorry I caused trouble between you and your girlfriend. That was not my intention."

"I know." I tossed one of the purple carrots up as we approached the grazing herd. "It's not your fault. Plenty of relationships don't make it long distance. I guess ours was one of them."

The herd noticed us and The Sergeant stopped so he could position himself between us and the other unicorns. He snorted softly, his ears flicking back and forth as he assessed the threat.

"Just us," I told the stallion, stopping with a good distance between us and the herd. It was always important to approach wild animals with caution and even though the herd was used to us, there was always a factor of risk when dealing with them.

The Sergeant sniffed the air and with a flick of his tail, he turned around to graze again.

Felicity chuckled. "Looks like it's safe to approach. He's such a good lead stallion."

"He is, isn't he? He takes really good care of his herd. I hope he won't mind us stealing Jun-Jun for a bit."

She tossed some of the purple carrots towards the group and immediately, the unicorns abandoned their grazing patch in favour of their favourite treat.

"I don't think he'll notice," Felicity noted dryly as she wagged a carrot towards Jun-Jun.

Since she was the oldest of the group and not in a position to challenge the others for her pick, she eagerly came our way. Sometimes, it was really incredible what we could achieve with these trained animals.

"Here, Jun-Jun," I called, also waving a carrot. "Come here, girl. I've got a treat for you!"

We lured the mare back to the working area where Nissan was waiting with the bucket of carrots.

"Well done," he praised us as he closed the fence behind Jun-Jun. He secured another gate, dividing the working area into two. One for the elderly mare, one with access to the stables where Sticker was waiting impatiently.

Felicity and I made our way out of the working area, finding a good spot where we both whipped out our notebooks. Pen in hand, I waited eagerly for Nissan to release Sticker. I was curious to see how the two would react to each other. If this meeting went well, there was a good chance we could integrate Sticker with the herd. If we were successful, that meant he had a new home. If not... He'd have to be transferred to another sanctuary or zoo with another herd. It meant saying goodbye to my newest friend.

With bated breath, I waited. Teasingly slow, Sticker trotted out of the stable, much more relaxed than when he arrived. His coat was healthy and shiny, his weight back to normal, and his confidence levels were up. We'd done a great job caring for him and it would be a terrible shame if the herd didn't accept him. Unfortunately, there was only so much we could control and influence. In the end, the animals got last say and if they didn't want to accept Sticker, there was nothing we could do to change it.

I really, really hoped that wasn't the case.

"There he goes," Felicity muttered. She made

some quick notes on her empty page and clicked her tongue. "This will go well, right?"

I nodded. "Jun-Jun is such a lovely, gentle unicorn. She gets along with everyone in the herd. I can't imagine her being nasty to Sticker."

"But we have no idea how he's going to react. There's a chance this will trigger a bad memory. Or if he has dominant traits, he might clash with The Sergeant."

"I'm sure it'll be fine. They've been able to hear and smell each other at night and we haven't seen any increased dominant, guarding behaviour from him." I nibbled on the end of my pen. "Oh, there they go."

Sticker noticed Jun-Jun on the other side of the pen and he approached her immediately, his young brashness shining through. Curiously, he pressed his nose against the fence and snorted softly to get her attention.

Interesting. I'd have thought he'd be the reluctant one but it looked like it was the opposite way around.

On the other side of the fence, Jun-Jun paid no attention to the newcomer. She chewed on her purple carrots, ignoring his impatient trampling.

Felicity snickered softly. "Aww, it looks like he's desperate to go over there."

"She doesn't want anything to do with him. Bless him. Poor boy."

"Look, he's hitting the fence. Wow, he's really eager to meet her."

Sticker proved her observation by neighing for Jun-Jun's attention. He paced up and down the fence, displaying more and more. Not that it was working.

Calmly, Jun-Jun finished her carrot and moved on to the next.

"Come on, Jun! Stop being so greedy and go say hello," Felicity encouraged the elderly unicorn.

The mare looked up from the bucket, stared us straight in the face, and continued chewing like she couldn't hear us.

"I think she's enjoying eating her treats in peace," I noted, scribbling it down in my notebook.

Felicity nodded. "I think so too. Maybe a small oversight on our part. Oh, but look. She's working on the last carrot. Hopefully, she'll give Sticker some attention after that."

A smile made its way to my face. I didn't like to admit it but this was a lot of fun. Observing unicorns in the beautiful sun, sharing notes with Felicity about my favourite animal. These were things that I wanted to do my entire life. Things that Tina never really understood. I'd always told myself that it was fine, that we didn't need to share that passion.

But being surrounded by all these people that lived and breathed animal care, I could tell that I wanted someone that loved it too.

I glanced at Felicity, noting the shimmer in her eyes as she watched the two unicorns in the working area. Her forehead was wrinkled in concentration and her hand clasped tightly around her pen as she took notes of the entire encounter.

That was what I wanted. Someone that loved this just as much as I did, that didn't make me feel bad for dedicating my life to it. And unfortunately, that wasn't Tina.

SIXTEEN

After Jun-Jun took her sweet time eating her treats, she finally made it over to the fence to say hello to Sticker. The colt trampled his hooves excitedly, eager to see another unicorn. Considering they were herd animals, the loneliness must've made it extra hard for him.

"There you go. Come on, Jun-Jun," Felicity muttered under her breath. Her eyes were locked on the unfolding scene and her nose was wrinkled in concentration.

She looked kind of cute like that.

I drew my attention away from the other girl and back to the meeting unicorns. They were gingerly sniffing each other through the fence, the gentleness a very promising start. If all the meetings went like this, we'd have a happy herd in no time.

While the two were getting acquainted, I noticed that the rest of the herd was coming this way. I assumed they noticed the upheaval and wanted to investigate why one of them was missing.

"They've come to look for Jun," Felicity observed. "Fascinating."

"I know." I flicked through my notebook to the page dedicated to the herd and made a note of it. "You can tell Sunshine is on a mission."

The lead mare paused in front of the closed working area and brushed her head along the fence. It was unusual for them not to have access so it was probably confusing, especially cause Jun-Jun was on the other side of the fence.

Nissan appeared out of the stables, the excitement written on his face. He joined us by the side, his voice elevated. "It's going so well. I'm really pleased with that."

"Do you think we should open the fence so Jun-Jun and Sticker can meet in person?" I asked. "Well, in unicorn."

Our mentor thought for a moment. "Yes, we should take advantage of the situation. Let's bring

Jun-Jun into Sticker's pen. If that goes well, we can bring in another herd member and another. As long as there's no aggression."

We all jumped in action, taking to our positions. Since controlling the herd was the most dangerous task, Nissan went to control the working area gate while Felicity and I brought the two unicorns together.

Excited, Sticker bounced over to Jun-Jun. He approached her a little too hasty and she kicked her back legs at him. A fairly normal warning, nothing to be too worried about.

The young colt calmed down and kept a bit more distance in his next greeting. He snorted softly, his ears up nice and high. He trotted over to her and bowed slightly, all signs of friendly behaviour.

Both unicorns seemed perfectly calm and relaxed, which was a great indicator. While they were getting to know each other, Nissan opened the gate and allowed Candle into the pen. Before the rest of the herd could follow, he engaged the lock, giving the filly a chance to sniff out Sticker for herself.

She gave him barely a glance before turning away, not interested in him. In this case, indifference was better than aggression. From either of them. She was only young so there was a chance he'd try to dominate her. But Sticker only had eyes for the elderly Jun-Jun.

Nissan seemed happy with the encounter too as he let the other unicorns into the working area. Distracted from fawning over Jun-Jun, Sticker trotted to the fence to meet the others. The twins beat The Sergeant to the fence and the three colts bucked energetically.

Maybe it was me, but it looked like they were excited to have another playmate.

My hands were getting clammy from watching the unicorns meet. Confident Sunshine approached the fence, chased the twins aways, and waited for the colt to greet her. She kept a close eye on his every move, her body language clear she was a bit more tensed than Jun-Jun. She had to be. It was her who maintained peace in the herd so bringing in a trouble maker would hurt their chances of survival.

Sticker seemed to understand the gravity of the situation too. He approached slowly and brought his nose up to hers. The two unicorns sniffed each other gently in their first greeting.

Standing next to each other, the difference in power was crystal clear. While Sticker was by no means a small unicorn, he was a skinny youngster compared to the mature Sunshine. Her proud horn highlighted the stump on his forehead and I had no doubt she would win if there was ever a scuffle.

She snorted softly and turned away, no longer interested in the young colt.

I breathed a sigh of relief. That was excellent. She seemed confident that he wasn't a threat, otherwise she wouldn't have turned her back to him.

Immediately, Sticker's playful behaviour changed. He lowered his head and seemed much more reluctant to approach the fence.

"He knows who's boss," Felicity remarked between notes.

"Clever boy. If he can get her approval, that's half the battle won. Now it's just The Sergeant's verdict left."

As soon as the words left my mouth, the stallion stomped over to the fence. Immediately, Sticker froze as he observed the other unicorn. If he looked small compared to Sunshine, he was no match for the buff and powerful Sergeant.

The stallion pressed his snout against the fence and exhaled loudly. His ears flattened slightly and the herd instinctively gathered behind him.

"Oh, oh. That's not good," I mumbled.

Felicity sucked some air between her teeth. "Don't be mean, Sergeant."

I wiped my hands on my uniform, not able to look away. If The Sergeant rejected him, there was no hope for Sticker. He'd never be able to fit into the herd without the lead stallion's approval.

The two unicorns were frozen in their stand-off. The Sergeant snorted loudly and scraped his hoof along the floor, hitting the metal fence. The loud bang spooked the young colt and Sticker darted back a few steps.

"Aww, poor Sticks," Felicity made another note. "I hope he can convince the Sergeant."

With caged breath, I watched the exchange. The Sergeant looked pleased by Sticker's reaction and with another puff, he stopped his intimidation. Sticker trotted back to the fence, carefully avoiding eye contact with the stallion.

From his post, Nissan gave us a thumbs-up. Instead of coming through the working area, he chose another exit and walked around as he joined us.

"That was tense," I blurted, not able to stop glancing at the unicorns. With the fence dividing Sticker from the herd, there wasn't much harm they could do but I was still worried. He needed a family and I really, really wanted it to be here.

"But it went well," Nissan concluded. "We'll let them get used to each other for the rest of the day and separate them at night again. But I think tomorrow, we can let them mingle."

"So exciting," Felicity exclaimed. She clicked her pen and made another note.

Interested, Nissan leaned in. "You two made a lot of notes. Can I see?"

My ears burned as I handed him my notebook. I never intended for anyone else to read my thoughts but I wasn't going to say no to him.

Nissan flicked through my pages and paused on the notes I made about Jun-Jun's abscess. "This is very detailed. You even wrote Jacob's observations down."

I nodded. "I wanted to make sure Jun-Jun's hoof healed up the whole way."

"Nice." He handed me my notes back and took a look at Felicity's. "I'm impressed. These are both excellent. Research is a big part of being a keeper so stay observant."

A sense of pride welled up in me as I clamped my notebook against my chest. His approval was really important to me, and considering his opinion would determine if I could stay here after my internship, this was really promising.

I glanced at Sticker and the rest of the herd. He wasn't the only one trying to find a new family and if I kept this up, maybe I'd get accepted just like him.

SEVENTEEN

Usually, after a day like this, I'd be giddy and excited to tell Tina everything. Except today was a bit different. We were in the middle of a fight and my recent realisation meant I had an uncomfortable call ahead of me.

I thought of all kinds of things I could do to put this off, but that would only prolong the misery.

Reluctantly, I pulled out my phone and dialled Tina. Surprisingly, it only took two rings for her to pick up.

"Hey."

I gulped. Tina didn't sound nearly as angry as I expected, but I could tell from her tone that she wasn't happy with me. Not that I could blame her, I did kind of hang up on her. For good reason, but that didn't change that we left things on an awkward note.

"Hi." I drew a nervous breath as I sat down on the side of the bed. "I think we need to talk."

Tina sighed. "I hate when we fight."

"Me too," I admitted, picking at my lip. I'd never broken up with anyone and this was Tina. I thought we were end-game. I was convinced about that until a couple of hours ago, but the denial had worn off. We hadn't been happy for a while and we were too different.

"I think the distance is just making me a little crazy. I've got a weekend off coming up. Maybe I should come visit you."

I picked at my lip. "I don't know. I'm really busy and I don't have any free days."

"Can't you just ask for one?"

Irritated, I kicked the edge of my carpet. "I can't just demand time off whenever I want it."

Tina sighed. "Alright, maybe I'll come anyway. I'll pretend to be a visitor. Then I can see those unicorns you're always talking about. You can give me a tour, show me around."

"You do realise if you visited when I'm working, I

can't really spend any time with you, right? I can't just let you come into the staff areas, that could get me fired." My frustration grew in my chest and I huffed. "Anyway, that's beside the point. I don't think you should visit."

"What? What are you saying?"

"I..." I gathered a deep breath, trying to find the courage to do what I had to do. "I think we should break up."

The line stayed silent for a couple of seconds before Tina reacted. She released a dismissive scoff. "Are you serious?"

I flopped down on the bed and pulled my pillow over my eyes. "I'm sorry..."

"You're breaking up with me over the phone?"

"How else would I do it?"

"You could've come see me in person?" she argued.

I put my phone to my other ear. "If we were seeing each other in person, maybe we wouldn't be breaking up."

There was some stumbling and the line crackled. "Fine. If that's what you want."

"I'm sorry... I'm just not happy and—"

"Whatever. Have a nice life."

The line clicked and I winced. I knew that the break-up wouldn't be well received but I thought Tina would've cared more about that than the manner in which I did it. She hadn't even protested, not that I wanted that, but it just confirmed what I knew. Our relationship was over.

Even though I broke up with her, it still sucked. I hugged my pillow, letting the loss wash over me. It was sad that we hadn't managed to make things work. But I also felt relief that it was over. The past weeks had been stressful enough and our deteriorating relationship had only made things harder. The relief also came with guilt that I felt this way about the end and continued to weigh on me for the rest of the week.

Every now and then, Felicity asked how I was doing but I didn't feel like talking to her. Instead, I just kept to my chores. The keepers at the meadland unicorn ponies seemed really happy with Aaron's performance so they'd requested his transfer. That meant he was guaranteed a permanent position after his internship. While I felt a little jealous and overlooked, it meant I didn't have to see his arrogant face daily anymore, so that was a perk. It also meant better chances to stay on with the silver blushes after my internship. I felt a little less excited about the prospect of beating Felicity to it but I couldn't let our recent friendship get in the way of my dreams. I had to be callous and keep my eyes on the prize.

I swept the broom through the stables, collecting all the stray dust and straw. It was a beautiful sunny day and combined with the weekend, it meant more visitors than usual.

Next to me, Felicity finished logging the daily checks while she whistled a soft tune. She was wearing her long blonde hair in a loose ponytail instead of a tight braid today. It made her look more approachable. Looks could be deceiving.

I glanced over to the meadow where the herd was grazing. Sticker included. He stood out as the only unicorn with a horn and he was still finding his place in the hierarchy, but it was all very promising. He just needed some time to really secure his spot but for all intents and purposes, he had a new family.

We did it.

A warmth welled up to my chest as I watched the herd out in the meadow. It had been hard work, a long process with no guarantees, but we really did it. Even if that was all I'd accomplish here at the sanctuary, it was still worth it.

A shadow fell over me. "Whatcha doing?"

I smiled, no longer deterred by Felicity's presence as I used to be. "Just admiring the unicorns. I'm really proud of Sticker."

The other girl joined me by the railing. "They look peaceful together. Sticker fits right in."

"He does. I think he's going to be really happy here."

"Happier than in the wild?"

I thought about that for a moment. "I'm not sure. The wild is dangerous and stressful. But it's where he belongs."

"Yeah. Hmm..." Felicity gave me a friendly shove. "Speaking of the wild, ready to get your freak on tonight?"

"Tonight? Oh, right. The Jungle." I reached for the broom again. "I don't know if I'm in the mood to party."

"Come on. You're a free woman again. Dancing and drinking is the cure for a broken heart."

"I don't know. It's just not my thing."

She raised an eyebrow. "Really? Could've fooled me. Didn't you win phoenix cup last time?"

I blushed. "That's different."

"Come on. Don't make me go with just Blake and Ramona. They're so going to hook up and I don't want to be a third wheel. Or worse, be alone with Aaron."

Surprised, I paused sweeping. "Blake and Ramona are a couple?"

"No, but I heard rumours that she's got a big crush on him."

"Huh. Did not know that." I thought back to all the times I'd seen them together, trying to work out if there was chemistry or not. "I don't see it. They don't have that vibe."

"You also thought I didn't vibe like I'm into women and that's not correct," Felicity remarked. With a confident tap and swipe, she traced her signature on the tablet. "There. That's me done for today. I'm ready to get out of here."

"I'm almost done."

Felicity leaned against the railing. "I'll wait for you."

I glanced at her, not sure if I heard her correctly. "Why?"

She clicked her tongue as she pushed herself up. "You make a good point. Byeeee."

She turned her head as she rushed out of the stable so I didn't get a good look at her, but it looked like she was blushing. Nah, Felicity wasn't the type to blush. I was making things up.

With a couple more sweeps, I finished my last chore for the day as well. On the way to the locker room, I thought about the Jungle. Partying wasn't my thing but it would be fun to hang out with my friends and I could do with blowing off some steam.

I nodded to myself. I wasn't sure if I had a good outfit for tonight but I'd figure something out. I was going clubbing!

EIGHTEEN

I didn't bring a lot of dresses with me. I wasn't really a dress girl either but I wanted to look good and feel confident. Like someone that was happy to be single and not my usual, frumpy self.

Unsatisfied, I glared at my reflection. All the hard work at the Sanctuary had bulked out my arms and the dress didn't look quite right anymore. Under different circumstances, I might have gone shopping, but we were going clubbing. It wasn't like anyone was going to notice in the dark.

I smoothed out the sides and pulled my leggings out of my crotch. Not comfortable at all but I wasn't confident enough to go without. Then again... Dark. Club. Who would notice?

No, I couldn't go without. That was too revealing. And too cold. I'd just have to put up with the discomfort.

A quick look at the clock left me just enough time to run a brush through my hair before I ran out of my room. As I put my key in the lock, I heard the door behind me open and I turned, facing Felicity.

My eyes widened and I couldn't help but do a double-take. Instead of the usual shapeless overalls, she was wearing a little black dress that really accentuated her curves. The heels made her legs look endless and for once, I didn't mind being looked down on.

"Wow." I held back the urge to whistle. "You look... not awful."

As soon as I said it, I could feel Felicity's eyes burning holes in me. "Aren't you good at giving compliments," she remarked sarcastically. "How did you even get a girlfriend in the first place?"

"By not giving her compliments?"

The other girl shook her head as we made our way to the elevator. "You're so clueless. I sincerely hope you won't use that line later when you're trying to hit on someone."

I pressed the arrow down. "I'm not going to hit on anyone."

"Because you're so bad at it?" she suggested. She

chuckled when I glared at her and gestured to the opening doors. "After you. See, now that's how you impress a lady."

"Well, I wasn't trying to impress you," I grumbled as I stepped into the elevator. The mirrors at the back and sides really highlighted how frumpy I looked next to the gorgeous Felicity. It was a good thing it was only a short ride down to the ground floor where the other interns were waiting. Aaron was leaning against the wall, flirting with some girls from the haggis habitat. Blake and Ramona were chatting between the two of them and I lingered, trying to figure out if Felicity was right about them being a couple. They looked cosy together, but nothing I wouldn't expect from friends.

I joined them and a handful of other interns from various other habitats. The air was crackling with anticipation and the excited chatter was putting me in a good mood. Maybe a night out was exactly what I needed.

A black cab was waiting just outside the campus grounds which took us on the short drive to The Jungle. The pounding music was audible from way outside and plenty of people were streaming into the club.

The other interns cheered and poured out of the

car, singing and dancing on their way in. I turned to check if the fare had been paid and found Felicity swiping her card to make the payment.

"How much is it?" I asked, rummaging through my little handbag for some cash.

Felicity shrugged. "No idea. I just swiped my card."

I followed her to the entrance of the club. "What? You didn't ask how much it was? Are you rich or something?"

The other girl made a non-committal noise as the bouncer stamped our hands with a colourful jungle print. "Shall we go dance?"

"Felicity. Felicity?" I hurried after her, bracing for the flashing neon lights. There was a heat inside the club from the dancing bodies and a distinct smell that I could only contribute to alcohol and sweat.

I spotted the other interns making their way to the bar, eager to spend some of our hard-earned money. The wage we got at the Sanctuary was small, especially as students, but we didn't have a lot of free time to spend it so on the rare occasions that we did, it flowed freely. Still, that didn't explain Felicity's blasé attitude to paying for the cab.

Unfortunately, the deafening music made it impossible to keep conversation so I just bobbed along with the music. Ramona handed me a drink before she went off to dance with Blake, potentially confirming what Felicity said earlier about her crush.

Everyone seemed more than happy to dance and sway along with the music. I wasn't exactly comfortable but I followed suit, bobbing my head to the rhythm of the deafening beat. To my left, Aaron whispered something in the ear of one of the girls, making her laugh over the top loud.

I didn't understand why guys like him were so popular but both the haggis interns seemed very interested in his attention. Gross.

Holding back a little gag, I took a sip from my drink and gagged for real. That was some terrible, terrible beer. It was worse than the cheap stuff we'd been drinking in the dorm and I had no doubt they were charging us a fortune for these. This was why I didn't like clubbing. But being sour about this place wasn't going to help me have fun either.

I took another sip, better prepared for the taste, and tried to focus on the music. The other interns looked happy to be dancing so I joined in, hoping I wasn't making a fool out of myself.

The hours passed surprisingly fast and the drinks flowed freely. I wasn't quite sure how many I'd already had but the liquor was passing straight through me. My bladder insisted I made a trip to the bathroom and there wasn't much I could do about that.

On my way back from the facilities, I spotted a tipsy Felicity in the queue with a strange look in her eyes. Once she saw me, she abandoned her spot and danced over to me. "Hey."

There was a slight husk to her voice that sent a little shiver through me. "Hi."

She paused in front of me, standing much closer than necessary. I took a step backwards, bumping into the wall. Felicity followed, her intense gaze never wavering.

"What are you doing?" I questioned, raising my arms to push her away. I put my hands on her hips, only realising it felt like an invitation when she leaned in even more.

Her warm body pressed against mine as she pinned me against the wall. The haze in her eyes brought a softness to her face that made her look so different from the usual concentrated and focused girl I worked with.

"Felicity?" My voice came out as a mere whisper. I wasn't quite sure what was happening but the few drinks I had were slowing down my thoughts. That didn't stop my heart from hammering through my chest as she rested her fore-head against mine.

"You infuriate me," Felicity murmured softly. She brought her face closer to mine, pausing for a second to brush a strand of hair behind my ear, like she was making up her mind about something.

I traced a finger up and down her back, enjoying how it made her close her eyes. She sighed softly as she cursed under her breath.

Before I could ask what that was about, she captured me in a kiss. Her warm breath and full lips against mine sent a twinge down my body and I could feel my hands travel from her hips to the small of her back. I'd barely kissed her back before she pulled away and left me stunned as she disappeared into the bathroom.

I touched my tingling lips, my mind racing to make sense of it all. Did that really just happen? Felicity... kissed me?

Unsure what to do, I lingered for a little longer before returning to the dance floor and rejoining the group of interns. Surprisingly, Ramona was making out with some random guy while Blake was nowhere to be found. At least Aaron was living up to his repu-tation and grinding with the two haggis keepers.

I swayed along to the music, not sure what was

supposed to be fun about clubbing. Nobody could talk to each other because of the loudness, I didn't like dancing, and it was too hot in here. I would've long gone home if it wasn't for...

Felicity.

I spotted her coming out of the bathroom. She made her way straight to the bar where the bartender served her immediately. She disappeared from view for a moment as two dancing guys broke my line of sight. Next I knew, she was standing next to me with a tray full of shot glasses.

"Shots!" she shouted, passing around the tray to eager hands. Once all the other interns had grabbed their drink, she presented me with the last one. "Shots, Charlotte."

I took the little glass while keeping a close eye on her. She wasn't paying any extra attention to me, considering we just kissed. Was she just playing it casual or did she already regret it? Was it a bad kiss that made her lose interest? I didn't even realise she was interested. Her behaviour certainly wasn't making that clear.

So confusing.

I joined the group in taking the shot and the alcohol stung the entire way down. I suppressed a cough as I put the empty glass back, glancing at

Felicity again. If she did it to get my attention, it certainly worked. So why was she ignoring me?

Why did I care? Up until the kiss, I hadn't even considered her as someone to be interested in. We were barely friends, what were we doing making out? And why had it made me weak to my knees?

The music changed and a slower song blasted out of the speakers. Immediately, people grabbed a partner to slow dance with. Ramona was still lip-locked with her stranger while Aaron was focusing his attention on the shortest of haggis keepers, leaving the second girl with a jealous scowl on her face. That was going to be fun for them tomorrow.

I glanced at Felicity but she had somehow ended up in Blake's arms. It didn't look romantic but then, what did I know? She slept with Aaron and she didn't like him. Maybe that was just the pattern. She didn't like me either so maybe that was why she kissed me.

Somehow, that stung more than expected.

Frustrated with the situation, I turned away and aimed for the exit, ready to get some fresh air. It had been hours since we arrived and the late evening had well and truly turned into a chilly night.

A handful of people were gathered around the club entrance, smoking, chatting, making out. The bouncer seemed to observe it all with a stoic disinter-est, especially since a girl an arm length away was puking her guts out in the gutter. The music was perfectly audible outside so I crossed the street so I could sit on some stairs. I reached for my phone and scrolled through potential listings for a cab. It wasn't a long walk home but I didn't fancy doing it this late at night. Considering that I had an early start tomor-row, I probably should've gone back to the dorm hours ago.

I ordered myself a taxi and waited for it to arrive, phone in hand. Some part of me expected Felicity to come looking for me, but she never did. Part of me wanted to text her I was going home but that felt like admitting I cared that she cared.

When the cab arrived, I messaged Ramona that I was leaving and called it a night. The entire drive home, I could still feel Felicity's lips on mine. Maybe if I'd been a little braver, I would've not cared about her indifference and kissed her this time around, but I didn't want to misread the situation. Maybe Felicity mistook me for someone else. Maybe she just wanted to kiss someone. Maybe she kissed me for my lipstick. Who knew. The girl was a mystery and I wasn't going to break my head over it. Besides, I'd only just gotten out of a dysfunctional relationship, I wasn't going to jump into another one.

The car stopped, jolting me out of my thoughts. I paid the driver, wincing at the fare. With a sigh, I swayed my way into the building and waited for the elevator. The metal door slid open and my dishevelled reflection was even worse than when I left. Perhaps it was a good thing that I'd gone back on my own so nobody had to see me in this harsh light.

I held onto the railing for stability and returned to my room, falling face-first into my bed. I was asleep before I hit the pillow.

NINETEEN

Morning came way too quickly and had me wishing I didn't drink as much. Or at all, for that matter. Why did I think clubbing was a good idea again? I'd set out with the intention of only having a drink or two but that quickly turned into a drink or six. What a terrible, terrible mistake.

I got ready for my day, trying to ignore the occasional bile rising up. Quieter than usual, I left my room and glanced at the door across. There was light coming through the crack underneath and I heard slight stumbling. Not ready to face Felicity, I hurried out to the elevator. Why did it feel like a walk of shame? Not that I had much experience with that.

The wobbly ride on the shuttle to the Sanctuary proved a real challenge for my stomach and I felt like throwing up when I finally got out. I recognised some of the interns from last night and they gave me a weak wave as they went on their way. At least it wasn't just me that was hungover and in awful shape.

I gathered a deep breath before I entered the stables, hoping to hide from Nissan that I was feeling terrible. While I was confident that I'd be able to get all my work done like usual, I just didn't feel like chatting, gossiping, or anything that required a bit too much energy.

"Morning!" I waved at my mentor, hoping to sound chipper.

He looked up from his phone and chuckled. "Hungover, huh?"

"What?" I thought about denying everything but he didn't seem mad. "How did you know?"

"I heard about the intern night out. You don't think you're the first lot of students to party it up, right? As long as it doesn't impact your work, I don't care in what state you show up" He scratched his beard. "Although it's probably better to avoid the public seeing you like this. Looks like you're on stable duty today."

The barn doors shrieked as Felicity dragged herself in with the same fake cheeriness.

Bemused, Nissan shook his head. "Should've known. Guess you're both on stable duty today."

Great. A whole day with Felicity was just what I needed.

I glanced at her but she wasn't paying any attention to me. What was her problem? What kind of person kissed another person and then ignored them after?

Maybe earlier, I was confused and curious about what it meant. Now I was just pissed off. She couldn't just kiss me, make me feel all these things, and pretend it never happened.

My frustration stewed during the unicorn's breakfast routine, growing and growing until I could barely keep it in. It wasn't until the herd was out grazing in the meadow and we were cleaning out the stable that I couldn't stay silent anymore.

"So... Last night, huh?" I remarked, trying my best to sound casual as I collected the dirty straw in the wheelbarrow. Last time we talked something out, we flung poop at each other but that was not going to be the case today. I wasn't that uncivilised.

Felicity grumbled. "I'm not in the mood to talk."

"Really. So you're just going to pretend nothing happened?"

She stopped shovelling and shot me a confused look. "Pretend... about what?"

I rested my foot on the pitchfork, my hand tightening around the handle. "That's cowardly. You can just say you regret it. Or that you were drunk and it was a mistake. I don't care. But that's just rude."

The other girl scoffed. "I don't know what you're talking about."

I resisted the urge to scream. "Whatever. I guess I've got my answer."

"Answer about what? Just tell me what you're talking about."

"No, if you don't remember, it doesn't matter." I scooped the last bit of dirty straw into the wheelbarrow and threw the pitchfork on top. Without looking at my source of frustration, I grabbed both handles so I could wheel it out.

"Charlotte." Felicity grabbed me by the wrist, preventing me from storming out. "Can you stop being such a woman and just tell me what's your problem?"

"You!" I thudded the wheelbarrow down. "You're my problem. How dare you kiss me and then just... not care?"

Felicity released my wrist like it burned her. "What? We didn't kiss."

I scoffed. "Ummm, yes, we did. Last night, you pressed me against the wall on your way to the bathroom. You kissed me, with tongue, I might add. And you don't even remember? You're such a piece of work."

I pushed the wheelbarrow out before she could add more insult to injury. I wasn't sure what was worse, that she kissed me and gave me the cold shoulder, or that she just didn't remember. Ugh. Why did I even care? It wasn't like I liked Felicity. The opposite, in fact. I actively disliked her. The way she acted like she was better than me, or how she always argued with me, or just her face. It didn't matter that we kissed because I had no interest in repeating it.

After unloading the wheelbarrow, I paused to look at the herd. Sticker was happily grazing with the rest of the unicorn, looking like he'd always belonged. The cheeky twins seemed happy to have a new playmate and Candle was slowly warming up to him. Every now and then, she followed him around in a way that made me wonder if she was developing a little crush on him. She definitely never paid this much attention to Criss and Cross. Sticker and Candle were both young but definitely mature enough to produce foals. It would be interesting to see, especially since Sunshine and The

Sergeant were long past their prime. If Candle ended up pregnant, it was possible that the entire hierarchy would change. Maybe the herd would even break apart.

I leaned against the railing. Not even unicorns could escape drama. While a little foal would be an amazing addition to the sanctuary and for the species' survival, it sucked that it could come at the cost of peace. I guess only time would tell.

A shadow fell over me and even without looking, I knew it was Felicity. She remained silent as she joined me to look at the herd.

Eventually, she spoke. "Is it just me or does Candle have a thing for Sticker?"

I sighed. This was what frustrated me the most about Felicity. The fact that she was actually good at her job and gave me a real run for my money. It would be easy to ignore or dismiss her if I didn't believe she'd be running her own habitat one day. While I was running my own, of course.

"They're so beautiful," Felicity mused. "Aaron is missing out. The meadland unicorn ponies are cute but they're just not... this."

"Aaron wouldn't know a good thing if it hit him in the face," I agreed, drinking in the quiet, peaceful atmosphere.

Felicity chuckled softly. "Did you see him making out with Sara?"

"Is that one of the haggis keepers?"

"Yes. Her sister was not amused."

I gasped. "No. They're sisters?"

"Yeah, they grew up on a haggis reserve so they're basically experts even though they're still students. Their internship is mostly for show, everyone knows they'll be offered a permanent spot."

"Tssk. Meanwhile, I have been working my ass off. The world isn't fair sometimes."

"Yeah." Felicity drummed her fingers on the railing. "I'm sorry I don't remember our kiss. I was... so drunk. I don't really remember how I got home."

"Can't help you there. I left on my own."

"Ah." The other girl let the tense silence hang between us as she searched for what to say. "I'm not very good at this."

"No kidding."

She clicked her tongue as we observed the herd. "So... Did you kiss me back or was I a complete ass?"

My cheeks grew hot as I avoided making eye contact with her. Somehow just answering the question felt like admitting something, even if I wasn't exactly sure what.

I could feel Felicity's gaze burning in the side of

my skull. With my eyes firmly locked on Sticker, I replied. "You weren't a complete ass."

Felicity released a smug little hum. "Aha."

Irritated, I glared at her. "Don't let it get to your head. I was really drunk too."

She met my gaze, her expression unreadable. "So you're saying it was a one-time thing?"

Why was she so blunt? I thought I spoke my mind but she was worse. And she was supposed to be the eloquent one as well. So how could she ask me all these things outright while keeping her own cards close to her heart?

Before I could formulate an answer, I heard a sound behind us as Nissan joined us by the railing. He looked out into the distance at the unicorns and nodded. "Looks like our Sticker is fitting right in. You can always tell whether a new member gets accepted into the herd if they're all peacefully grazing together. I think Sticker is going to be very happy here."

"The Griffin Sanctuary is a great place to be," I responded.

Nissan nodded. "It is. Speaking of... Charlotte, your evaluation is today."

I froze. "What? I thought it wasn't until next week."

My mentor shot me an apologetic smile. "It's been moved forward. Come to the meeting room A after your break."

"O-Okay..." I exchanged a look with Felicity, not managing to keep the worry from clouding my thoughts. My evaluation was brought forward? That was not good news. Was this because I came in hungover? But Nissan said it was fine if I didn't let it affect my work. I thought I hadn't but... the timing was suspicious. He hadn't said anything about Felicity's evaluation though. Did that mean it was only a problem for me? Or had they already decided to kick me out?

I tried to get a read off of Nissan's face but the bearded man had a real poker face. He hummed while he did some tasks on the tablet, not looking like someone that just fired one of his interns. But that didn't mean anything...

TWENTY

My hands were shaking as I paced back and forth in the lobby, waiting to be called into the meeting room. While the previous evaluation had been stressy, it wasn't nearly as nerve-wracking as this one. What if this was it? What if this was the end... I didn't think I'd performed badly but compared to Aaron and Felicity... Maybe I was the weakest of the three.

No, I couldn't think like this. I'd worked so hard. Too hard. This couldn't be it. This was my dream.

After what felt like forever, the door ahead swung open and Gwen waved me in. I followed her along the blue carpet and took a seat in the wooden chair, trying to stop my leg from shaking.

Gwen took place at the table, where Director Starlise and Director Ella were waiting. Both of them were here... Whether that was a good sign or not... I wasn't sure.

Ella clicked her pen a couple of times and tapped it against her chin. "Charlotte... Why did you want to work with the unicorns?"

A little confused, I considered her question. It wasn't that I had to think hard about the answer, I'd known that for years, I just assumed this was something they'd ask me when I submitted my application.

"I saw my first unicorn when I was seven. It was here, at the Sanctuary, with my mum. I remember her telling me to pay attention because that might've been the first and last unicorn I'd ever see. It broke my heart and I just thought that if we worked a little harder and came together, we could do better." I took a breath, trying to contain the stream of words. "I guess I never let go of that childish dream and when I got the opportunity to intern here, I just knew I had to give it my all. I've been giving it my all."

The two women exchanged a look and Starlise continued in a strong but gentle tone. "We're very happy with your performance. However, the interns we have this year are really strong and unfortunately, we have a limited capacity."

Tears welled up in my eyes but I blinked them

away. I didn't want to cry. I couldn't cry. This couldn't be happening. Was I really hearing what I was hearing? Was this their way of saying I wasn't measuring up against the others?

I balled my hands, trying to contain my emotions. I would take this like a champion. I wasn't going to cry. No tears. No tears.

Ella flicked through her notes. "I see that you're graduating in zoology, but you have a veterinarian course as your minor. How come you didn't pursue that as your major?"

"Umm..." I cast my eyes to the floor. "I didn't get in."

"Your grades are excellent though," Starlise remarked.

I smiled through my tears. "I worked really hard for them. I wanted to prove that I could do it."

"I think that's become evident." The two directors conversed quietly as they exchanged some of their sheets. Starlise showed her wife something and surprised appreciation flitted across Ella's face.

I waited in pained silence. These women had my dream in their hands and with every passing second, the likelihood of being offered a job as a unicorn keeper dwindled away.

With a sigh, Ella folded her hands. "We think

you show great promise and aptitude. There's no doubt that you're smart and know your way around animals. But—"

There it was. The dreaded but.

"After your internship, we won't be able to offer you a permanent position as keeper," Ella said.

Before I could hold it back, a sob escaped. Hot tears finally spilt out and rolled down my cheeks. I tried my best to hold them back and remain dignified but my disappointment couldn't be contained. I'd worked so hard for this, I came so close. How did this happen? How did I mess things up?

I wiped my tears on my sleeve, sobbing and hiccuping as I tried my hardest to remain under-standable. "I understand... I'm really grateful for..." My voice hitched in my throat and broke. "Really grateful for everything. I'm sorry that I—"

"Look what you did, you made the poor girl cry," Starlise whispered to her wife. "I told you to lead with the other thing."

I wasn't sure how I heard her through my crying but I looked up, my vision blurry from the tears. "What other thing?"

"We can't offer you a permanent position as keeper but we'd like to turn your internship into an apprenticeship as a veterinarian assistant. We know that extends your studies and it's not the dream job you were hoping for, but we're hoping to be in a different position next year where we can offer you a permanent position. We think you'd be excellent at it and Jacob is happy to take you under his wing. He said you had the stuff, whatever that means."

I sniffled. "So I don't have to leave the Sanctuary?"

"No. The apprenticeship would last two years and you'll be tending to animals all over the Sanctuary so it'll come with a lot of extra studying. I know it's a lot so take your time to think about it."

I didn't have to. I sniffed the tears away and managed a smile. "I accept."

The two women seemed surprised. "Are you sure? You don't have to give us your answer right now."

"I'm sure. Working here is a dream come true so I'll work really hard so I can be a great veterinarian assistant."

Ella and Starlise smiled. "That's wonderful to hear. We'll make the necessary arrangements with your school and you'll get some more paperwork. We're really happy you're staying with us."

"Thank you." I wiped my eyes again. "Thank you so much."

With shaking hands, I turned around and made my way out of the meeting. This was not how I expected that to go and while this apprenticeship was a fantastic opportunity, it stung that they hadn't offered me a permanent position as keeper. It hurt. It really hurt.

Tears welled up just thinking about it and I pushed them to the back of my mind, trying to be happy about this. While it wasn't how I'd imagined things, I still got to work at the Griffin Sanctuary.

Determined, I nodded to myself. I was going to be the best veterinarian assistant they'd ever seen.

EPILOGUE

One week later

MY FIRST DAY of my apprenticeship felt just as nerve-wracking as when I arrived at the Sanctuary for the first time. I'd never have thought that I'd be eligible for a vet program like this, especially after failing my entrance exam and turning to zoology. And yet, here I was. Ready to put my skills and knowledge to the test.

Instead of going to the unicorn habitat like usual, I made my way to the building attached to the quarantine bay. That was where Jacob always started his day and now that I was his apprentice, that was where I was going too.

I swiped my ID at the gate and let the badge snap back against my chest. The change in routine was a little unsettling and I didn't really know any of the nurses or veterinary staff, but it couldn't be worse than working with Aaron and Felicity. Although I had to admit that I was going to miss working with her and taking care of the herd. I'd still see the silver blushes every now and then but my focus would be spread out between a much larger variety of animals.

I was way, way, way out of my depth so I'd have to learn quickly and adapt even quicker if I was going to make it.

With my entire body tingling with nerves, I paused in front of Jacob's office. The door was open but I didn't know if it was policy to just waltz in so I knocked.

"Come in," Jacob called in his deep voice. He looked up from behind his desk and smiled. "Ah, Charlotte. Good to see you."

"Thanks. I'm excited for my first day. And nervous."

My new mentor rose from his desk. "Don't be. Let's walk and talk."

He didn't have to ask me twice. I hurried to his side, eager to get started.

If Jacob noticed my eagerness, he didn't show it. He angled his tablet so I could see the agenda and all the appointments on it. "First thing on our agenda is a visit to the phoenixes. It's nesting season and Lander said he thinks they'll have their first eggs today. Do you know him?"

I shook my head as we left the vet block behind us. We passed the primary staff facilities and continued on to the phoenix house.

"That's okay. Over time, you'll get to know everyone. We work closely with a whole bunch of teams so it's really imperative to get along with everyone." He thought for a moment and tapped a couple of times on his tablet. "Have you been given access to the sanctuary's platform?"

We passed a group of floor crew on the path on our way to a part of the Sanctuary I'd only been to as a guest. "No, what's that?"

"An online space for everyone to chat. Usually, interns don't get invited but you're an apprentice now so I don't see the harm. I've sent an invite to your email address. You can introduce yourself on the forum and get to know everyone, even people that are on different shifts. It's very handy."

That sounded like a lot of peopling. Not exactly

my best skill but I had no choice. For a lot of animals, being well-socialised was often the key to survival. I'd have to adapt as well if I was going to make it through my apprenticeship and learn everything there was to know about the mythical creatures at the Griffin Sanctuary.

On our way to the phoenix habitat, I noticed a whole bunch of fire-hazard warnings and fire extinguishers. I turned to Jacob to ask about it, but a loud phoenix honk trumpeted through the quiet morning, followed by a panicked scream and a deafening alarm. A gust of fire shot up through the fence of the aviary, setting some of the plants and trees ablaze.

"Oh shit." I grabbed one of the many fire extinguishers and raced into the building, ready for whatever new adventure was waiting for me.

THANK you for reading The Unicorn Herd. I hope you had a lot of fun with the unicorns, the Griffin Sanctuary, and all the people caring for the animals. There's still a whole lot more to explore so join Charlotte as she gets to know the phoenixes and the other mythical beasts.

Read The Phoenix Nest here: https://books. arizonatape.com/thephoenixnest

Or you can pick up a free prequel where Charlotte goes looking for fairies here: https://books. arizonatape.com/ioo2nkhq6x

ABOUT ARIZONA TAPE

Arizona Tape lives her dream life hanging out with her dog and writing stories all day. Her favourite books to write are urban fantasy and paranormal romances with queer leads, stories that she wished were around when she was younger.

When she's not writing, she can be found cooking up a storm in the kitchen, watching shows that make her cry, or trying her hand at her new hobby of the week.

She currently lives in the United Kingdom with her girlfriend and her adorable dog who is the star of her newsletter.

Sign up here for adorable pictures, free books, and news about her books: www.arizonatape.com/subscribe

Follow Arizona Tape

Website | Newsletter | Facebook | Facebook Group |
Bookbub | Twitter | Instagram | TikTok

- https://www.arizonatape.com
- https://www.arizonatape.com/subscribe
- https://facebook.com/arizonatapeauthor
- https://facebook.com/groups/
  arizonatape
- https://www.bookbub.com/authors/
  arizona-tape
- https://twitter.com/arizonatape
- https://instagram.com/arizonatape
- https://www.tiktok.com/@arizonatape

Here are some recommendations on some of my other books you might like. My books are available on all retailers and can be requested in most public libraries.

You can find out more about each of my series on my website: https://www.arizonatape.com

Crescent Lake Shifters

Take a leap of faith with these dragon shifters looking for love. Only a jump in the Crescent Lake will reveal the bonds of fate. A paranormal romance series. Each book follows a different couple.

The Griffin Sanctuary

Help Charlotte take care of endangered mythical animals in the Griffin Sanctuary in this urban fantasy series. Perfect for animal and mythology lovers.

Queens Of Olympus

A modern paranormal romance take on the Greek gods and their dating life; it's not *all* drama. Each book follows a different couple.

Crescent Lake Bears

Jump in the lake of love with these bear shifters looking for their fated mates. Only the crescent moon will reveal what's meant to be. A paranormal romance series. Each book follows a different couple.

Guardian Of The Winter Stone

A fast-paced epic fantasy romance about a lone wolf shifter and her two fated mates on a quest for redemption, honour, and a sacred relic that holds the secrets about her past.

Amethyst's Wand Shop Mysteries

An urban fantasy murder mystery series following a witch who teams up with a detective to solve murders. Each book includes a different murder.

Purple Oasis

Find love and hope after the apocalypse at a sanctuary for witches, shifters, and more in this paranormal romance series. Each book follows a different couple.

For a full comprehensive list of all my books: www. arizonatape.com/all-series

Signed Paperback & Merchandise:

You can find signed paperbacks, hardcovers, and

merchandise based on my series (including stickers, magnets, badges, and more!) via my website: www. arizonatape.com/shop

My website also has a selection of free stories and books that'll give you a taste of my other works: www.arizonatape. com/free

Printed in Great Britain
by Amazon

45314660R00138